A Future With Brighter Days

A. M. Howcroft

Copyright © 2025 A M Howcroft
The moral right of the author has been asserted.

Cover design by InkTears
with original image from Midjourney

Apart from any fair dealing for the purposes of research or private study, or criticism or review, as permitted under the Copyright, Designs and Patents Act 1988, this publication may only be reproduced, stored or transmitted, in any form or by any means, with the prior permission in writing of the publishers, or in the case of reprographic reproduction in accordance with the terms of licences issued by the Copyright Licencing Agency. Enquiries concerning reproduction outside those terms should be sent to the publishers.

InkTears
5 Story Ln, East Sandwich, MA 02537
ISBN 978-1-910207-22-2

Contents

Mutilated Gods 4

End Of The World 15

Gingerbread 23

Time Travel For 11-Year-Olds 32

The Flavours Of Savannah 39

368 Friends 50

The King's Men Vigilantes 58

The Twaddlers Of Newport Beach 69

Wild Animals 81

Fragile 88

Laughing At Funerals 95

Butterfly 108

Blue Monsters 121

Shadow Day 128

One Page Ahead 139

Other People's Wives 150

When We Were Gone Astray 166

Race For The Pot 177

This Is Not How It Ends 184

Made In Morocco 200

Acknowledgements 208

A Note From The Author 210

Questions for a Book Club 214

Mutilated Gods

Friday night beckoned, but Sue planned on retreating to her flat and savouring a couple of ice-cold Stella's. Another few stripes and she would finish the manor lawn. Tipping the grass cuttings over the wall into the compost, a faint breeze wafted tiny green shards across her face, where they stuck to her skin. She mopped her brow with a dirty forearm and tightened the scrunchie in her hair, as she walked past the twin statues of female elegance guarding the maze entrance. Around the yew-hedge corner she was surprised to see a man standing there. The Dennetts weren't due back from Tuscany for a fortnight.

"Are you Sue, the gardener?" he asked.

"Who are you?" Sue demanded.

"Conor — the house sitter," he said warily.

Sue vaguely recalled Mr. Dennett mentioning someone would be here.

"Yeah," she took off one glove. "I'm a bit sticky." His palm felt cool.

"I was looking for Ares," Conor said.

"You mean Juno?"

"No, not the dog. It's a statue, male, muscular, eight or nine-foot tall. Ares, one of Rodin's mutilated gods. I thought it would be easy to find but he seems to be hiding."

"Books and classical stuff's not really my specialty," Sue said. "I'm better with my hands." Her face turned red, and she swivelled. "I think I know the one you want, though. This way." She led him to the maze entrance and explained the directions.

The lawn's neat lines pointed invitingly towards the horizon, as Sue rolled the mower into her van. Pulling off her gloves, she inspected her fingers and their chipped nails. She was ready for a beer. Sue knew it was hard to leave the maze though, if you didn't know the route. The house-sitter seemed friendly, but Sue told herself she wasn't his type, she wasn't anybody's type. It wasn't only gods that got mutilated.

When she stepped into the central square of the maze, she saw Conor's head lowered, as he concentrated on his drawing to render the hard lines with swift, bold strokes. He worked rapidly to capture the shadows that gave the stone its dominating presence. Ares was brooding, powerful and aggressive. She called Conor's name.

"Over here," he replied.

Sue edged closer to steal a glance.

"What do you think?" he said and held out the sketch for her to see.

"I'm not much into art," she said.

"Really?" He nodded at her tattoo-covered arms.

"Yeah, well, I didn't draw them."

"You chose them, which is equally important. Is that a lily?"

Sue twisted her arm around and held the skin taut. "It's a dog-rose, and it's only a half-sleeve, but I might go full. The writing says alis volat propris. Which means —"

"She flies with her own wings," Conor said. "Beautiful. And that?"

"Fourth Mechanised Brigade. Those are my tour dates." She let her arm drop, suddenly self-conscious.

"Why house sitting? she said.

"It's fun staying in exotic houses but I'm not sure I'd want to own one. I like the freedom to go from place to place. As a bonus, I get a stream of interesting things to draw." He looked at her.

"I get it," she said.

"Is that your handiwork?" Conor pointed to a daisy chain around the ankle of Ares.

"It's plastic. I think Mrs. Dennett put it there."

"You know," Conor said, "The Greeks chained their statues to the temples."

"So they wouldn't get nicked?" Sue said.

"It was to stop the gods escaping. The Spartans had Aphrodite chained up, after they heard what happened to the Greeks. The statue of Athena fled the city as Xerxes and his army drew near."

"I'm not going to judge anyone for running from a battle," Sue indicated the subject was closed with a shift of her body.

"You didn't say what you thought of my drawing?"

Sue smiled. "I like it. You've captured the scale. Why are statues so much larger than life?"

"Perspective. The intended audience were looking at it from a distance, and they needed something impressive. The Americans didn't invent shock and awe."

"You don't think they're huge because the gods were bigger and stronger than us? Like it wasn't art, but fact?"

Conor said, "There were even larger statues. Cicero saw the colossus of Zeus and said, *the more one looks at it, the bigger it seems to become.*"

"Fear can do funny things," Sue answered.

For all the time she'd spent trimming the hedges, Sue had never looked closely at the warrior in the middle. The arms and chest were gigantic, like the biggest specimens she'd met in barracks. The pose was one of contained energy, dynamic, like bottled anger ready to explode, or perhaps implode. The hair was curled tighter than springs, and the eyes were gouged holes filled with emptiness. She reached out and impulsively ripped the plastic daisy-chain off Ares's ankle.

"Nobody should be a prisoner," she said.

They stared at the statue, as though waiting for a reaction. Sharp-angled shadows were shielding much of his torso and only a raised fist and a calf muscle were lit. The silence throbbed, reminding Sue of the feeling that follows a patrol down the wrong street.

"Let's go," Sue said.

"You should give me a ball of string next time."

As they turned the corner of the house, something small shot past them into the archway.

"What was that?" Sue asked.

"It looked like a hare, or a pheasant."

Sue thought that those two animals should look very different. They walked to the arch, and it reappeared, a small bronze figurine, perhaps a foot high. It wore a helmet, bracers on each wrist, plus small boots with tiny wings that fluttered and twitched like an engine on idle. It spoke in a surprisingly loud voice with a high pitch, like an over-excited child. The language was unintelligible.

Sue swore several times in disbelief. Conor's mouth was wide open. The figurine waited for an answer but since none came it reeled off another burst of gibberish.

"It's speaking Greek," Conor said.

"What's it saying?" Sue asked.

"I don't speak Greek."

The figurine paused again, waiting for another answer.

"Yassas," Sue said.

"I think it must be ancient Greek, like Olde English. It won't understand the modern language."

The figurine screwed up its face and spoke a handful

more staccato words and pointed over to the right and then it was gone, darting away like a bronze dragonfly.

"Well, I think I could make a rough translation of those words," Sue said.

Following its indicated direction, they walked back around the corner to face the maze. A new, rough-hewn path had appeared, with shattered twigs and a carpet of leaves. An empty pedestal was visible. Huge indentations marked the freshly mowed lawn, and a path was beaten through the barley that filled the vista beyond the ha-ha wall.

"Impossible," he said.

"Nightmare," Sue replied.

"We should call the police," Conor decided.

Sue put on her telephone voice. "Yes officer, we've lost a Greek god that goes by the name of Ares. He has a flying bronze pet with him."

"Point taken," Conor said.

"Let's find it." Sue ran towards the ha-ha, diverting briefly to collect a broom. She placed two feet on the brush and bounced as though she were on a pogo. After the brush popped off, she twirled the five-foot pole.

"Weapon?" he said.

"More like a cattle-prod. I don't think we'll win a fight."

The path arrowed straight towards the woods. Sue set off running, following the ready-made trail.

"What's it doing?" she asked.

"I don't know," Conor was trying to keep up with her fast pace. "Food?"

Sue thought about that and smiled. She recalled what she'd wanted most when arriving back from a tour, and it hadn't been food.

"It wasn't asleep," Conor shouted, since Sue was

getting further ahead.

She slowed down to let him gain ground, and a little respect. "What do you mean?"

"The Greeks believed that gods could come in and out of their statues. Their power could be divided without diminishing. They could be in Olympus, several temples, on a battlefield all at the same time. Something's brought it here, into the statue," he finished.

They were at the wood's edge where branches of oak reached out over the barley, and the sun was setting ahead of them. The dark trees had never looked less inviting.

"What are we doing?" Conor puffed.

"Maybe it needs our help."

"It's a god, a marble giant. They take whatever they want. We don't speak Greek and the light's failing. Going into these woods is suicide."

Sue looked at Conor.

"It isn't courage if you're not afraid. I pulled off the daisy chain, so this is my mess."

Sue stepped forward, and Conor followed.

The woods were dense, and they were collecting scratches from a multitude of splintered branches. Sue emerged first into the clearing. The sky was blood red, outlining a small faux temple on the hill's peak above them. A black shape loomed up next to it, scaling-out until it seemed to fill the sky.

"My god," Sue murmured.

"No, this is somebody else's god. The Christians thought the Greek statues were filled with demons."

"Great!" she whispered.

Ares turned towards them, advancing in rapid strides.

"Don't run," she said. "It might chase us like a dog."

"If it can smell fear, we're in big trouble," Conor

answered.

Ares was speaking in a melodious, deep voice, and Sue wondered if he was talking to himself or them. The sounds were beautiful, like the melody of a chain-smoking lion. As he approached, Sue grasped the pole in both hands, shifting her weight and stance.

A grey figure rushed out of the woods to their left.

"On your right," Sue said, and Conor glanced the other way to find a second statue going past him, one of the two that usually stood sentinel at the maze. The females advanced towards Ares, armed with a spear each. They were smaller than Ares and made of stone rather than marble but converged fearlessly on their target. The huge god stopped and boomed out what was surely a command. One of the females replied, in a quieter voice that reminded Sue of a burbling stream. Ares seemed unsure, shaking his head, and continued, rumbling like distant thunder. Sue noticed that the god of war had no weapon, but his hands were clenched into boulder-sized fists.

"Is it a negotiation?" Conor whispered.

The two female statues began to sing and hop from one leg to another, in what seemed like a dance. The sound was haunting, yet neither modern nor classical, wild and strangely synchronised. Ares leapt forwards. A spear was hurled from the left and he swatted it away with the outside of his forearm while simultaneously grasping the spear on his right and unbalancing the holder by dragging the spearhead from side to side. The spear-less statue on the left hurled herself at Ares and he grasped her arm and wrenched it high. Now, with a spear clutched on one side and an arm on the other, he twisted and turned as his wriggling captors fought back furiously. The statue on the right dropped her spear and swung her open hand. Distracted for a second, he missed the other statue who while still held high by her left arm swung the right hand into Ares's face. The crunch echoed off the trees and Conor flinched. The huge god staggered back, and since he still held the offending statue by one arm, he swung her with violent force into the other female, smashing the legs from beneath the advancing statue. Sue watched as the torso kept crawling on its arms towards her sister, seemingly unperturbed. The red sunlight showed a cavity where Ares proud nose had been. Ares was careful to hold the remaining statue high and wide now as he moved forward and stamped on the head of the advancing body, leaving a rocking torso behind.

The dangling statue thrashed her free limbs but seemed powerless to reach her tormentor. Ares chest heaved as he took her other arm so that he held both wrists. Then he began stretching his arms out wide, and she wailed. Ares expanded his huge reach. Sue covered her ears as the shrieks became unbearable. The right arm snapped off, leaving a twisted stub of metal. Grasping the woman by the waist for leverage, he continued to rip off the other arm before crushing it inside his marble fist. Hurling the body aside he turned back to Sue and Conor.

"I think this is our cue to disappear," Conor said.

"You think you could outrun him?"

"No. But he can't chase us both."

Sue watched the marble giant for a split second.

"Go!" she shouted. Dropping her pole, she threw herself into the trees, weaving around trunks and crashing through branches. Fear and panic chased every step. Something was wrong, though — she could neither see nor hear any pursuit and Conor should have been hurtling through the undergrowth to her side. She spun back towards the clearing, bursting through the trees to see Conor holding her abandoned pole, pointing it threateningly at the chest of the colossal figure towering above.

"You've read too many tales of Greek heroes," she shouted.

"They're all tragedies," he replied.

Ares swatted the pole dismissively, snapping it in two, and turned his back on Conor. In a handful of giant strides, he stood before Sue and boomed a command, loud enough to make her ears ring. Shaking her head, she held her hands out to either side in a gesture that, she hoped, conveyed a lack of understanding. Please don't rip my arms out of their sockets, she thought. His eyes were shadow-black and seemed to bore through her. With a thud Ares dropped to his knees, bringing the enlarged head closer to her face. His tone was lower, almost mournful. He looked to the sky and cried out. With a gesture, Sue signalled Conor to keep his distance.

"Where is she," Conor said, loud enough for it to carry. "I think that's what he said.

"She's not here," Sue spoke quietly, and shook her head as she repeated the phrase. Then she stepped closer, holding one hand out. Ares seized her hand.

"You're warm," she managed to say, and since Ares had made no move to tear off her arm, she held out the other. More gently this time, Ares took the second hand in his and turned both hands over. He leant forwards with the curled locks on his head sharp in relief. His eyes were black as the river Styx, but with a melancholic grey ring. A last trick of the failing light made the sun flare in those deep-sunk eyes. For a moment, Sue wondered if her independence and freedom from the old life was really all she craved. The narrative she had built for herself might be a lie.

Ares hands cooled and hardened. The chest stopped rising. Gently she moved one hand, and then the next, slipping them out of his marble fists. She stood on tiptoe and planted a kiss on the statue's forehead, then stepped back several paces.

Together, Conor and Sue surveyed the scene. The nose-less face of Ares was surrounded by scattered limbs, weapons and the torsos from the female statues.

"It looks like a battlefield," Sue said.

"Or a museum," Conor added.

Making their way back across the field in the twilight, a slight breeze cooled the air, and the crop whispered as they passed.

"They won't believe us," Sue said.

"Who?"

"The Dennetts, the police. They'll say it was PTSD."

Conor pulled at a spike of barley, and began crushing the grain in his hand, discarding the husk and inspecting the seed. "Then let's not say anything. I'll call them tomorrow, blame it on vandals."

"Who were the other statues? Which gods were the women?" Sue asked.

"I think they were handmaidens. Servants of Artemis or Aphrodite."

Sue shook her head. "Why were they fighting him?"

"They seemed to be defending you. I wondered, well…" Conor's voice trailed off into the murmuring barley.

"What?"

"I thought you might have seemed familiar to them. Like when you see a face in a crowd, and for an instant you think it's someone you used to know."

"Are you saying I look like a goddess?"

Conor coughed. "You have quite classical features, you know, like a straight nose, and, um…"

"Thanks."

They walked for a few more paces in silence, before

Sue spoke again.

"Shame we don't speak Greek. Imagine what they might have told us."

"You must have witnessed some pretty incredible stuff yourself," he said.

Sue shrugged.

Conor continued, "The Greeks didn't understand their own gods. All they knew was that they fall in love, make mistakes, fight, and suffer passions like the rest of us."

"We get the gods we deserve," Sue said.

"Do we still have any?"

"Exactly," she said.

The freshly cut lawn gave out its distinct smell of summer. Conor recalled the many Greek gods the modern world had abandoned, for lost shepherds, harvests, and drowned sailors. He wondered if there was still one lingering in the world, for second chances.

"Would you like a beer?" Sue said. "I've some in the fridge at my flat." She chewed her lip in the darkness.

"That sounds great," Conor replied. "Let me get my pad and pencils so I can pay for my drink with a portrait."

"You don't need to do that."

Conor smiled, "I know, but I want to."

Sue considered several replies that were witty or sarcastic. On another night, she would have used them.

"Thank you," she said.

End Of The World

Luke parked at the top of Vincent's Nob. The town lights were beautiful, but it seemed so clichéd that Susie was surely waiting for him to pounce. He switched the truck lights off and paused as their eyes adjusted to the night. He'd meant to leave the stereo running, with his carefully selected playlist delivering a message he couldn't say aloud. Susie opened the passenger door and hot air rushed into the vehicle. She walked around the truck and stood in by the radiator grill. He followed her. The stars, bright and scattered, mirrored Luke's chaotic thoughts.

"It makes you think, doesn't it?" Susie said.

Luke made some guttural sound, not sure what to say. He wondered if he should lean against the vehicle, and how close to stand. The gap felt awkward, although Susie seemed completely relaxed.

"About life, I mean," Susie continued. "We've worked so hard for our exams, and you look at this and wonder why?"

Luke leaned against the truck and slid as close to her as he dared. "I brought you here for a reason," he said. "We should witness something spectacular. Biggest solar storm since 1921, apparently."

"What will we see?"

"I imagine it'll be like the northern lights, but nobody's certain."

"Is it safe?" Susie asked.

He shrugged. His dad had ordered extra tanks of water and a backup generator to prevent a zirconium fire in the cooling ponds.

"My dad's freaked, but then he has a panic-attack if the vending machine runs out of coke zero. There is a tiny chance the reactor might blow."

"So, this is it, eh, end of the world?" Susie turned to him and Luke thought she was smiling in the dark. She seemed closer. "Just you and me left?"

"Could be," he said. "Although it would take some time. Basic electrical systems to start with, since we lose the grid first. Transformers and synchrophasers fried, probably the PLCs and the SCADA systems too. Laptops, cellphones, most cars, anything with delicate electronics. I wouldn't want to be in a triple-7 at 31,000 feet."

"Or underneath it," Susie said. She brushed his hand as it rested on the truck's bonnet.

He carried on talking. "No electricity across North America, food riots, looting, that's for starters. Then we get the real trouble. The cooling systems on the power stations fail. The cores shut down automatically, but the old fuel rods start to burn-out. Without electrically powered cooling it's only a matter of days before they ignite. Fukushima's all over the country. Chernobyl multiplied by a hundred."

Her hand was resting on his. Susie had turned her whole body towards him. She wrinkled her brow. "What about back-up generators — won't they kick in?"

Luke, carefully leaving his hand unmoved, said: "In theory they should, but they'll be affected like everything else, so at least half will fail."

"That means half will succeed," Susie said. "Positive thinking, Luke. Things might be better than you imagine." She squeezed his hand.

This was it. Every nerve screamed at him to turn and kiss her, but he was pinned down by the weight of years of inaction. For three years, he'd thought of nobody but Susie. If he tried anything, it might all go wrong, and he would lose his best friend, and everyone would learn about his humiliation.

Then again, there were only a few months before she would go to college, and he would be abandoned and forgotten anyway. He calculated that the risk/reward quotient was at the maximum tonight, but still he was paralysed. There was too much at stake. His eyes had dilated enough to make out her features, even in the semi-dark. That perfect button nose, above a wide, lopsided smile with a vicious half-life that meant Luke could be irradiated by a single expression for weeks.

"If it all ends tonight —" Susie said quietly, and Luke leaned closer.

The sky flared, a pink and violet flash that lit up the sleeping town and momentarily silhouetted the cooling towers. Susie jumped forwards. Luke felt his stomach lurch as her hand tore away. Another hesitation, another missed opportunity.

"Was that it?" Susie asked.

"I hope not," Luke said. She shifted her gaze back to him. For a second time the sky lit, this time in green and white, taking longer to fade.

"It's like watching lightning over the mountains. For once, I wish I could be right in the eye of the storm," Luke said.

From the town, a siren wailed like a banshee.

"Can it damage us?" Susie asked.

"No." He was positive about this. "It's CME plasma." Damn, he thought, that sounded geeky.

"CME?" Susie said.

"Coronial Mass Ejection," he said, taking care to enunciate the last word clearly, desperately avoiding a Freudian slip. "The plasma interacts with the outer atmosphere and the magnetosphere to deliver a GMD, that's a geomagnetic disturbance."

"Didn't they do that in Mission Impossible?" she said.

"In movies they use EMPs — same thing but man-made, more directional, and much weaker."

Susie walked a few paces towards the steeply sloped hill to stare down at the town, and the twinkling streetlights. Luke dug his fingernails deep into his palm, clenching his fist at his side. His chest tightened. This might be the last chance he and Susie would get to be alone together. It had taken hours of planning and a bunch of luck to get her away from their usual crowd, and yet he was busy trying to explain the difference between EMPs and GMDs. This was a repeating pattern, good planning then poor execution. He couldn't pull the trigger when it mattered. Scooping up a stone, he hurled it into the darkness.

"Penny for your thoughts," she said.

"I was thinking... that I don't want to be smart, sometimes. I'd like to know less," and be more impulsive, he thought.

She laughed, "Hey, you don't know everything. I like you as you are."

Like, she'd said. Wrong word.

Fainter at first, but then with growing intensity, a brilliant aurora began to dance across the sky, illuminating the mountains. They stood in a comfortable silence for several minutes, each gazing at the stunning display.

"It makes you dizzy," Susie said. She sat on the grass and Luke copied her, lying down beside her as she stretched out on her back. He watched the celestial fireworks and let his hand inch across the ground until he found hers. It offered no resistance as he took it lightly in his grip and stroked her fingers.

"Do you think we'll go blind?" She asked.

"What?!"

"Remember, book club with Mrs Panerone?"

"Oh, yeh. Village of the Damned?"

"No," she said. "And that was the film anyway. The book was called The Midwich Cuckoos."

"Day of the Triffids?" he offered.

"Correct, eventually." She twisted sideways. "See, you don't know everything."

"May be these are Martian landing craft," he said.

"Ogilvy the astronomer assured them that the chances of anything coming from Mars were a million-to-one. He was frackin' wrong though," her impersonated deep-voice cracked, and they laughed. Susie pushed herself up on one elbow and rested her free arm on his chest. Luke wondered if she could feel his heart pounding.

"Listen," she said.

Luke could hear nothing but her breathing and the galloping of his heart.

"I want to tell you something — don't get up," she pushed his chest back into the grass. "My plans have changed. I wanted you to know before the others. I move to Colorado next week."

"When?"

"Tuesday," she gave him a micro sad-smile.

"You'll miss the summer party," he managed to stammer. Another flare lit the sky. Susie ignored it and pressed her index finger to his lips.

"Shhh," she murmured. "I know. It's the end-of-the-world. We've had such a great journey though." She stopped to search for the right words.

Luke wanted to argue, to beg her to stay, but the words were tangled in his heart. If he spoke, his voice would break, and all he could manage was to hold still and try not to show any reaction. He fought to control his feelings.

"This is the end, Luke. We both know it. If we start

something now, it will only damage the future. You've got things to do here. I don't want you putting your life on hold, and I can't either. I'm not explaining myself very well. You understand, don't you?"

It was his turn to speak, but he felt hollow. Even a single word might be fatal. The sky was mercifully dark again.

"Speak to me, Luke," Susie said, and rubbed her hand across his chest.

He lay on the flint-dry grass, immobilised. She slapped his chest, lightly, as though trying to restart a faulty device. He decided to tell her the three words that were always a mistake. The words that can never be taken back. He opened his mouth, but all that emerged was a mangled groan. Tears began streaming down his face, and he struggled to get air into his lungs and regain some semblance of control. The embarrassment was devastating, but the loss hurt more. He imagined himself drifting through space, with no oxygen, the earth receding into a tiny blue dot.

Susie squeezed closer and brushed her hand across his forehead then used both thumbs to wipe the tears from his cheeks, without saying a word. For a few minutes, neither of them spoke.

"In 1859," Luke finally said, "there was a geo-magnetic disturbance they called the Carrington Event. The induced currents were so high that telegraph lines set on fire, burning trails that seared across fields. Modern systems are much more sensitive and vulnerable. Nobody knows how much damage they might take from this storm. They might never recover."

Susie kissed him on each cheek and his forehead.

"There's always a positive, remember? What could you do Luke, to protect the grid?"

He thought about the question, ignoring the subtext.

"Well, there are Hall-effect sensors that can check if a transformer is at risk, but they're too expensive to put everywhere. I've always considered that a GMD might be managed by monitoring synchrophasor data in real-time. The patterns may give enough localised warning to flick the switch, like a circuit breaker, without having to do expensive field assessments or relying on vulnerability reports. That should provide enough protection to bring the grid rapidly back to life."

Susie pulled him reluctantly to his feet.

"Look," she said. The town lights were out. A few beams from creeping cars edged around the streets, and it looked odd. "People like you can use a disaster to make things better, stronger. This isn't Armageddon, it's a new beginning."

He smiled. "It looks reasonable now, but when the coolant boils off the discarded rods, and the zirconium fires start, and some idiot tries to throw water at them, well, BOOM!"

"Exactly," she said as they got into the car. "There will be another explosion. It takes two idiots though, not just one."

Luke fired up the engine. They took one last look across the town, and the nuclear power station leaning over the suburbs.

"So this is what the end of the world feels like," he said.

"Did you think it finished with a big bang?" Susie's double entendre was deliberate, and he laughed.

"I wonder what the probability would be, for the same universe to form a second time?" he said.

"Infinitesimally small." Susie answered, then softened her words. "But you never know. I suspect the new universe will be just as amazing."

They began the descent back to a changed world, each

quietly calculating an unpredictable future, spun from random collisions and remote possibilities. Above them, the lights swirled in crimson and violet, a carefree chaos, too beautiful to last. It felt as uncontrollable and hard to grasp as everything Luke had wanted to say.

"When dawn comes, the aurora will be gone," Luke said.

"No," Susie answered. "It will still be there, even if the daylight means most people can't see it. You and I will know the truth."

"Always," Luke said, shifting into a higher gear.

Gingerbread

A set of plastic ramekin dishes full of candy are laid out down the centre of the table. There are multi-coloured m&ms, liquorice, chocolate logs, peppermints, tubes of ready-made icing, and round chocolate balls that are officially reindeer poo. We skipped the gumballs, which are a nightmare for false teeth, and the snow-like powdered sugar, because that was certain to end up over someone's new Christmas hairstyle. The gingerbread sets are cheap at the local store, and Donna collected a handful. She's certain the patients will know what to do.

"They always remember kiddie things," Donna says in her strong accent, towering over me. She wears flat shoes but still has to duck under the lights. She looks more like a wrestler than a nurse, but the two roles have more similarities than you might imagine, in here.

Only Mabel, Alice, and Lulu show any interest in the activity. I confess, I've never made a gingerbread house. I didn't realise you stick the walls and roof together before you start decorating, or how hard that can be, for three women with diminishing hand-eye co-ordination.

"Don't squirt that into your mouth, Mabel!"

I guide her hand back to the ridge of the house, where we're attempting to stick the roof on. The walls are already leaning against each other like a drunk on a lamppost, and the amount of white icing we're deploying to plug the gaps recalls my miserable attempt to re-grout the bathroom tiles. I glance at Lulu, but she's quiet, and rarely causes any trouble. Lulu has lost the power of speech, at least anything that makes sense. Although, she does love to be hugged. Most of the day Lulu cuddles her stuffed Dalmatian toy. For ten minutes, I keep working with Mabel, sticking sweets on the eaves of her lopsided house.

"Lulu!" Donna cries.

I swing around, holding Mabel's wrist to restrain her from spraying liquid jets of sugar. Lulu seems oblivious to her name and continues decorating her creation. She hasn't built a gingerbread house; it's a rectangular mansion in a Baroque style. There are at least twenty windows on each of the four main floors, and on the front face she's adding a handmade sugar clock in the centre, directly above the doorway, which is constructed from pillars of liquorice.

"It's a work of art," Donna declares.

Even Mabel stares at the incredible building. It looks like Lulu has opened several packets of the basic house kit and broken rectangular walls and roof pieces to make the long shapes for her structure. Then she's piped the windows in place. There are grooves on each biscuit, to help children see where windows and doors should be, but Lulu has ignored these, making her own designs in white, criss-crossing over the underlying patterns.

"What is it?" I ask Lulu.

She says nothing. As I said, she can't talk anymore. With total concentration, she continues piping more details.

"Well, it's not her old home," Donna says. "She lived in Peter's Street," she nods in the vague direction of that part of town, where the houses run together, fifty at a time, in one long row.

As soon as it's built, Lulu drifts away.

***

By late afternoon, all the staff have seen the gingerbread mansion. We lead Lulu into the lounge at dinner, but she doesn't give her construction a second glance.

"She reminds me of one of those talented autistic kids," Donna says. "Wasn't there one boy who could draw any building, like an architect?"

"Yeah, memory is funny." I say. "None of the patients can recall what happened five minutes ago, and yet they can describe the street where they went to school."

"That's the damaged hippocampus. They can't process information to store new memories," Donna says confidently.

Everyone wants to know if Lulu's creation is a real place. Unfortunately, there are no relatives on file for Lulu, she came via Social Services. We take some photos of the building instead, and Donna wants to post them on Instagram, but the manager doesn't want the press attention. Before my shift finishes, he calls me into the office.

"I know what it is," he says, and turns his computer screen around. There's a photo of a building with orange-coloured walls and hundreds of windows. The lowest layer seems to be built from a different coloured stone.

"Yes, that's it," I say. I'm even more amazed. Lulu has created an astonishing facsimile of this place, purely from memory.

"It's the Lubyanka," the manager says darkly.

"The lub..?"

"Lubyanka. It was built for the All Russian Insurance Company, and then requisitioned by the Cheka, the Russian secret police. Headquarters for the KGB."

We're both silent, trying to register the meaning of that.

"What do we know about Lulu's background?" I finally ask.

He sighs. "Very little, I went over the paperwork. There's a list of addresses going back thirty years, it looks like she moved here from Birmingham in the late 80's."

"Place of birth?"

"We don't even know her age, for certain."

"I think Nina speaks some Russian?" I say.

"Lulu's way past language of any type."

***

I can't sleep. What if her husband or son were taken to Lubyanka, never to return? Or had she been a spy? When a person's memory has withered, and all that remains are childhood scraps, how can a building be so perfectly recalled? I marvel at the dexterity and skill with which Lulu pieced it together. Was she once a sculptor? I imagine all the things she could have told us, if we had talked earlier, and asked the right questions.

***

In the morning, I stop by the arts and crafts store. I buy a pad, coloured pencils, and one of those fine black ink pens. There's something inside Lulu that wants to come out, and I'm determined to help.

Donna has already fed and washed Lulu, who is sitting in her armchair. She smiles as I enter the room, but as a polite, courteous reaction. I never get the sense that she can distinguish me from the other nurses.

"Lulu," I sing her name softly, as a mother might, "Do you want to draw?"

I kneel beside her and gently place the pad on her lap, putting a blue pencil in her hand. She grips it, and looks down, puzzled. Guiding her hand onto the paper, I move the pencil around, letting her feel the weight, as blue lines swerve across the page. I take my hand away and abruptly, she stops. I try another couple of times, but to no avail.

Hearing my name called, I go where I'm needed, leaving Lulu with the artist's materials. One task leads to another, and it's an hour before I return. She's sitting peacefully. The pad and pencils have fallen to the floor. I pick the pad up, hopeful, but there's nothing except the blue swirls we made together. I notice the black pen grasped tightly in her hand and have to prise her fingers open to remove it. Then I discover that the walls and bed sheets have been scribbled on, with indelible black ink.

"Oh Lulu…" I groan.

These are not amazing pictures, simply the scribblings of a toddler. Repeated circles, and x's, or perhaps badly drawn t's, or even a religious cross. Looking for anything of meaning, I wonder if some lines are meant to represent an H, drawn over and over.

"Isn't H pronounced like an N in Russian?" I wonder aloud. Lulu smiles, but she smiles whatever I say.

***

The next day I resolve to try again. I stop by the supermarket where the gingerbread kits are reduced in price and buy a couple. Donna and I fashion the identical layout, using the same room and sweets. Mabel and Alice are no longer interested, but four other patients come to raid the candy, causing mayhem. Distracted though we are, Donna and I keep a watchful eye over Lulu. To begin with, she simply opens the packets and eats some gingerbread. Donna rolls her eyes. Next time I check, Lulu is frantically busy.

"Donna," I command.

Lulu is breaking the gingerbread into shapes, and

shuffling them, like a jigsaw puzzle. She chunters away, a stream of meaningless words and sounds.

"Does that sound like Russian?" Donna asks me.

"More like gibberish."

Lulu grabs the tube of icing sugar and glues pieces together. At first, I assume it's random, since the shapes make no sense, there's nothing emerging from the triangles and squares she has made. Then Lulu places a corner down, turning it the other way up, and I realise her model was upside down.

"It's a church," I say.

Donna's mouth is wide open. It's another fabulous model, with tiny arched windows, and a steeple that's coming together magnificently. This is the work of a professional artist, a talented sculptor at the top of their game, not a ninety-year-old woman with arthritis and Alzheimer's.

"You better get the manager," Donna finally says.

I don't move, fascinated by Lulu. I watch the speed of her fingers, and the confident assembly. She pipes another clock-face, drainpipes, a religious cross with a figure, showing an intricacy that makes her last effort seem feeble. Finally, she steps back, and with one swipe, hammers the steeple, smashing it into the table.

"No, no, Lulu," Donna cries out, and we grab her arms to prevent Lulu doing any more damage. She puts up no resistance, and looks at me and then Donna, bewildered. Her lips move, moistening, as though she's preparing to speak, but the words are lost somewhere in the labyrinth of her mind, and her eyes show disappointment as the words slip away.

"Now why did you do that, Lulu?" Donna cajoles her. "It's beautiful. You've got hidden talents."

The manager spent hours trying to identify the church,

looking for a clue to her identity. It was an impossible task. There are thousands of churches, all seemingly based on the same styles and shapes. That night I searched the web myself, then watched TV, eventually falling asleep on the sofa.

My bedside alarm rings in the distance, but it's my vibrating cellphone that wakes me. I have a terrible crick in my neck. There are seven messages, all from Donna. Her last text says BBC News, now. I turn on the TV, and there it is, a stone and glass version of Lulu's gingerbread church. The steeple is a smouldering ruin. The reporter smirks as he talks about an act of god. He turns to a local, who claims to have seen the devastating lightning strike. The reporter signs off from outside of Carcassonne, in the south of France. The final shot is from a helicopter, circling the site. I go cold, because the ruins aren't similar to Lulu's replica, they're identical.

***

It's now Christmas Eve, and I know the shops will be crazy, but I must buy more gingerbread houses, to see what Lulu will do next. I walk along the seasonal shopping aisle, scanning rows of chocolate Santa's, and cut-price panettone, but I can't see any gingerbread. A hassled-looking member of staff tells me everything is out on the shelves. I improvise by collecting flour, ground ginger, cinnamon, brown sugar, some eggs, a jar of syrup, and a batch of cookie cutters and tools.

Donna and I are rushed off our feet for most of the morning. Visitors piling in to get their filial duty completed, so they can enjoy Christmas Day without guilt. The manager saw the news, but not the connection.

"Coincidence," he says.

I make the dough at lunch time, and give Lulu the

cookie cutters, and the left-over bits of candy from our previous day's baking. We're not sure how she'll cope with freshly rolled dough, but she begins cutting out shapes and decorating them. There's none of the frenzy from other days, but she seems happy making little stars and figures. She leaves a couple of pieces blank, squares and rectangles, and in between clearing the tables from afternoon tea, and running back and forth to lock or unlock multiple bolts that keep the residents secure, and let guests escape, I pop her gingerbread in the oven. Luckily, Donna hears the timer and pulls them out before they burn. She scoots them onto a rack to cool.

Next time I see Lulu, it's near the end of my shift. Donna has already gone home, as her family are arriving for the holiday. I wanted to tell Donna about the science program I'd seen the night before. There was some concept about a Möbius strip and parallel dimensions that had confused me, but the smooth-voiced narrator had said time wasn't linear. It was more like two dots on a piece of paper, and if you folded the paper, the dots might touch. He'd said yesterday and tomorrow could join, making the future seem like a memory. I wondered if an old person could mix past and future together until they became the same thing.

Lulu is in the dining room. Donna must have given her the icing tube and baked gingerbread, or she found them herself. She's built another house, smaller, a traditional home with gingerbread men around the edge. I'm partly relieved that it's much simpler, and a smidgen disappointed. There was something magical and mysterious before, and perhaps it's gone now, and we'll never know what Lulu was trying to express.

"Hot!" Lulu says.

I look at her in surprise, shocked to hear her first real word in months. She stares back, looking equally surprised.

"No Lulu," I say. "It's not hot. You can eat a piece."

I mime eating, and she returns to a state of confusion.

Snapping the head off a figure, I pass it to her, and she nibbles.

Then with a jolt, I recognise the building. It's our care home. The figures around the edge are angels. My hands shake as I realise that I can identify them. There's the manager, and Mabel, Alice, even Lulu herself, all in miniature. Donna is there. Her figure towers over everyone, as usual. The odd thing is that the building is crammed full of m&m candy, in bright colours — red, yellow and orange. My heart is racing. I look more closely at the figures. Mabel, Alice, and Lulu all have wings, and their heads are turned upwards and smiling. Donna's replica appears to be weeping, with her head bowed. I see that her figure has no wings. I look for my own tiny gingerbread-voodoo doll, but it's gone.

Lulu is crunching away, with crumbs on her chin. I see my gingerbread-foot disappear into her mouth.

"What does it mean?" I ask Lulu, trying to control the panic in my voice.

She licks her mouth and swallows. "Hot," she says again.

The deafening screech of the fire alarm rings through the building, and Lulu grabs my wrist, with a grip like a demon.

Time Travel For 11-Year-Olds

The New Year begins when a girl steps on my ear. Luckily, she's taken off her stilettos. They dangle from her hand, and if she was still wearing them, I'd be deaf as well as hungover. My reward for last night's party is a throbbing head and ear. I look around to see there are ten of us sleeping on the floor, curled and contorted like a flattened game of twister. My clothes are stale with smoke and my jeans have a dark stain, hopefully red wine, that wasn't there the night before. I slip away from the aftermath, convinced I know the way to the underground station. Twenty confused minutes later, I'm lost. The district looked different last night, swarming with lights and noise. There'd been flocks of girls in sequinned dresses, struggling to balance on dramatic heels. The roads seem quiet this morning, dilapidated and worn-out. I probably look much the same. If I keep walking, I should stumble across the tube. It's easy enough to find by drifting from lanes to streets, like following a stream to a river.

I could've stayed with the crowd, who were planning a hair of the dog. Took plenty of juice last night though, and besides, I need to let January's austerity wash over me, to cleanse the guilt of another year wasted. Time is more valuable than money.

The streets seem different in this part of town. The houses are ill-proportioned, like a giant has squeezed them together, cracking a few walls and making the paint peel, until the buildings appear thin but tall. I feel out of place. Even my skin colour seems the wrong shade. A couple of scruffy kids on bikes are watching me and laughing. There's another boy coming my way, wearing a geeky-green anorak.

"Hey," I say, stepping across his path to make him stop.

He says nothing, as though he's been taught not to talk to strangers with werewolf-red eyes. "Do you know where the nearest tube is?"

"Yes" he answers.

That'll teach me to ask closed questions. "Where is it?"

"It's not easy to explain," he says.

"Can you show me?" He looks uncomfortable, his face registering the clash between a desire to be the good Samaritan and parental advice on talking to crazies. He's wary. I decide to sweeten the deal.

"In return," I tell him, "I can teach you to time-travel."

"That's not possible," he says.

I crouch down low so I'm at his level, and talk softly, to stop the bike kids from overhearing. "Well, you're partially right." I tell him. "You can't go back. Nobody can erase their mistakes. You can go forwards, though."

"To see the future?" he says, not believing, but hoping. I nod slowly.

"Nah, you can't do that," he shakes his head.

"You can, once I've shared *the knowledge*."

Silently, I count to five, as his brown eyes bore into my throbbing head.

"I can take you as far as Bretchers Hill, it's easy from there. Deal?"

"Done," I hold out my hand and he shakes it, loosely.

We set off with the boy leading, immediately reversing my previous direction.

"Do you know those two?" I indicate the bike-kids with a head tilt.

"No," he says, without even looking.

We take a right, and then a left along a sweeping curve of street with even taller houses that seem ridiculously narrow.

I wonder if everything inside matches; thin arches, skinny cookers, a pencil bath, and willowy people. I vaguely recall Einstein's theory that if you travel at the speed of light, everything contracts, and time seems to stand still. When you get back to where you started, everyone else has aged.

"What's it like?" the boy says.

"Eh?"

"The future."

"You know, it's not so different. There are new bits of technology that are fun for a while. Not everyone you love makes it there, but you find new people. Pain, disappointment, loneliness, they all stick around."

"Doesn't sound that great," the boy says.

"Those are the futures I've visited. Yours will be much better. I've only ever gone there to escape the present."

The two bike-kids race past. The first boy has a mop of dark hair, and once beyond us he glides, so he can look back and stare, while the smaller kid with stubby legs pushes his bike from side to side as he strains to keep up with his bigger friend.

"This way," my diminutive guide says. We cross the street behind the bike-kids, who are circling at the bottom of the cul-de-sac, and we turn right.

"Why don't you use it now, to get where you're going?"

I tell the boy, "Smart question. The truth is, I don't use it anymore. Time travel is best for 11-year-olds."

"I'm eleven," he says proudly.

"Perfect." I glance back, and see the bike-kids, who must be thirteen or fourteen, tailing us. Mophead looks away when he sees me watching. He mutters to his mate.

"Why did you stop time-travelling?" The boy asks.

"Too dangerous. As you get older, it gets risky."

We weave through a few more streets, largely in

silence.

"This is it," the boy says. "I'll give you the final instructions when you've told me how to time-travel." He can't help but smile at his own cunning ploy. We're standing by an alleyway that seemingly stretches to infinity.

"What's your name?" I ask.

"Everyone calls me Jet," he says.

"Well, Jet, can you click your fingers?"

"Of course!" He's about to demonstrate, but I grab his hand.

"Not yet." I let go, and he rubs his fingers as though checking to see if I've stolen any. "Here's what you do. Let's say you're somewhere you hate —"

"Like where?" he interrupts.

"Ever had a filling at the dentist?"

"No, but I had a tooth out that was cracked," he pulls his lip down and points.

"Was it fun?"

"OK," he says. "I get it. Somewhere I hate."

I crouch low again, holding my finger and thumb as though I'm about to snap them together.

"When you're in that place, think of the spot in the future where you'd rather be. Like your home, say, and be specific about what you're doing. Perhaps you're listening to a certain song in your bedroom, yeh? Then click your fingers."

"That's it?"

I continue. "When you get home, or to the place you imagined, remember to click your fingers again, and you'll have travelled forward in time to that spot."

Jet shakes his head, clearly unimpressed. "It's a trick," he says, sighing. He points down the alley. "At the end, turn left, and the underground is five minutes away."

He walks off.

"Jet," I call. He looks back. "It's a trick, but it works."
He shrugs.

I head down the alley and hear the distant whoosh of two bikes. The passage slopes gently upwards. Mature trees overhang in several places, casting deep shadows. The sides switch between hedge, creosoted-fence and red-brick walls. The alley makes me feel claustrophobic. I look at my finger and thumb. When I was a boy, one click could rush me home if my brother was back from the city, get me through an injection, or a school trip on one of those coaches that roll like a yacht in the swell. As I got older, I jumped further into the future, bypassing a week on a boring training course, and on one occasion, all of March. That was the last time though, when I finally understood the danger. I tuck both hands into my pockets for safe-keeping.

I round a corner, and there it is. An Alsatian. A massive, powerful, black and brown monster. I've startled it. The creature's first response is to go stiff and tall, so every muscle pops out like a canine body-builder. Then it begins to growl, a low undulation with lips pulled back so I can see a pink tongue rougher than sandpaper and four, enlarged, yellow canine-teeth.

***

Jet knew the teenagers were following him. They had been since before he met the weird man. He'd hoped that a detour with an adult might have shaken them, but he was wrong. Now he was further from home, in an estate he didn't know very well. Jet climbed the steps of the rusting metal bridge that crossed the railway line. He could hear the clang of one boy's feet on the steps below. Glancing down through the open metal-lattice, he could see him bouncing his bike up the steps. Jet decided to run. He was nearly halfway across when the dark-haired boy appeared at the far end of the bridge, on the top level. Dark-hair began riding towards him, grinning. Jet stopped. Behind him, Stubby-legs reached the top level, lay his bike against the guard rail and began walking, slowly and with menace.

Dark-hair stopped his bike in front of Jet with a screech of brakes. "I don't know you," he sneered.

Jet said nothing, in case he chose the wrong words.

"Doesn't he realise this is our bridge?" Stocky-legs said from behind.

"Your bridge," said Jet. "What are you, trolls?"

He meant it as a joke but could tell immediately it was a mistake. He put his thumb and middle finger against each other and imagined a hot bath with steam clouding up the room. Then he snapped his fingers together. Nothing happened, and then Dark-hair lunged forward. The next few seconds were a blur. Jet was shoved against the chainlink fence and suffered a flurry of punches and kicks. Then Dark-hair was racing away on his bike, with Stubby-legs chasing after him on foot. There was an enormous crash, and Jet saw a bike hit the gravel on the railway siding, as though it had been hurled off the bridge. Turning around, he saw the weird man smiling.

"Luckily for you, I had to take a small detour," he said. "I saw it though — you time-travelled!"

"It didn't work," Jet said.

"Wait 'til you get home," the man replied.

***

His mum had wanted to call the police, but his dad said *best not to make a fuss.* The steam filled the tiny room, and Jet floated in the hot bath. He had a couple bruises and a scrape on his back. Otherwise, he was fine. He was trying to forget the whole day, but it was hard not to replay it and see how he could have acted differently. He suddenly remembered that the bath was his future place that he'd wanted to reach in the moment before the attack. He knew it was a trick but couldn't resist putting his fingers together and clicking. He waited a moment to see if anything had changed and laughed. There was no magic, no teleportation, but the man was right. It seemed like only a moment ago when he'd been standing on a bridge being threatened by two thugs, and yet he'd clicked his fingers and now he was here, exactly as imagined. The trick worked. Everything in between had happened, but it felt like it was gone. All that mattered were the two connected moments.

He submerged into the heat, leaving only the oval of his face above the water line. The world became a muted murmur, that could be operating at any time and pace without him. He felt safe.

I could click my fingers at school, he thought, and a double-maths lesson would be over. I could click my fingers, and it would be summer holiday. He felt his heart pumping inside his chest. I could click my fingers, he thought, and I could be an old man remembering how I learnt to time-travel when I was 11. When I'm old, he thought, it might be the only thing I can remember clearly, after my other memories have faded. He lifted his wrinkled hand out of the water and put his thumb and finger together.

The Flavours Of Savannah

Nostalgia was not our best-selling option. We would have stopped selling it years ago, but there was a niche that reliably came back for more. That was before the *Bad Times*. After that, it seemed we couldn't get enough. Nostalgia was the zeitgeist, and it didn't have the hard come-down of the high pleasure alternatives. The price rocketed, and raw materials got harder to source each week. Every guapo on the grid was mixing and selling, and we needed a way to differentiate. I told Savannah to focus her planet-sized brain on the issue.

"Why's it my problem?" she said.

"Our problem, but your specialisation. You know me, distribution, planning, ops. You handle product."

She made a sound that could have been an acknowledgement, or perhaps an indication that I was a total idiot and took a sip from her frozen sunset. I was on the juice.

"Besides, I can't take any more tofein," I said. "Tofein soup, grilled tofein and watercress, tofein quesadillas. I'm sick of it." The texture was driving me crazy. I couldn't complain about the taste, because it didn't have any. "I need meat. We gotta get some denaro flowin' again."

Night-shift deep in the levels. It was slippery-hot, and I was desperate to move, but Savannah was knotted into my arms with one leg thrown across me, fast asleep. Every forty minutes the gas-turbine one zone across would fire up like a jet engine, straining to pump out the nitro-oxides, sulphur, and CO_2, the nox, sox and cox as Savvie called them. She groaned in her sleep, and I shifted position to try and find a cool patch on our thin sliver of bed. Heaven and hell, it was both. Her scent drifted up to me, and she whispered,

"I can give them what they want."

"Who?"

"Everyone," she said, then sighed, and fell back to sleep.

How she dreamt up the flavours, I don't know, but they were her masterstroke, chemo-neuro-magic. Savannah's a genius but stays in the shadows. Dresses scraggy to hold the guys away and keeps her distance from the geeks, too. Savannah and me are tight. Got her out of a few holes when it all went bad, up there. Nabbed a crib in the levels when the exodus began. Nothing fancy, but better than those communal halls, with lice in the beds and broth.

You know, real nostalgia is a positive set of memories, polished by retelling, that conveniently ignores any nasty stuff. It combines with your understanding that things turned sour later, to give that sweet taste with a bitter hint. Like remembering that post high-school vacation with your crew. You recall it as everyone being carefree, filled with laughter and romance. The memory's pure and true, if you forget about the angst and hangovers. The bad part comes because you know what followed — the girl killed by a drunken bigot in a truck, the fluke injury that ended your best friend's sporting career, the drudgery of real jobs, all the dreams that died. That's where the nostalgia kicks-in.

What Savannah did though, was to make our Nostalgia more than a vanilla-sensation. She figured out how to tune it for vacations, love, sporting victories, winter, childhood. She found a way to kick in the right neural transmitters to trigger specific feelings. She called them flavours. They worked differently for each person, but they were much more targeted, and repeatable. We'd hit gold but it wasn't enough for Savannah.

My shop's pretty deep in the levels, as you'd expect. No sunlight, our vit-D all comes from supplements. There's no room to swing a cat, and if I had something that valuable, I wouldn't be whirring it around like an AC-fan. I have a sliding door of steel but when I'm here I leave it open and use a beaded curtain that rattles when a customer arrives. I'm normally reading, thrillers and stuff. Books are the most powerful drugs. I thank the stars they're not rationed yet. My shelves are stacked with jars that hold tablets, gels, and capsules of every shape and colour. I have no idea what most of them do. I picked them up as a job-lot. Occasionally, someone finds something they want, and I try to guess what they can afford, and we haggle. Most people don't come here for the pills though, they're to make us seem legit. People want real medicine; the stuff Savannah makes.

"I'm a chemist, not a criminal," Savannah says.

"You're an artist," I tell her.

"You're full of shit," she says, but I can tell she's flattered.

The problem with the flavours was that we needed ingredients you can only get from sub-surface level, where the fat-cats and politicos live. Getting into their zone was easy, because there were good reasons for nobodies to come through the gatehouse — fixing pipes, delivering food, repairing generators, whatever. The gatehouse didn't care either, it was only a job, and they were as depressed as the rest of us. Savannah and I knew how to get past them. That's not to say we weren't nervous, the first time. I was dripping with sweat even in the air-conditioned halls of that upper zone. I was shocked at how wide the connecting spaces were. The lanes, tunnels, and even the corridors, all felt like goddam freeways. You could have squeezed two Level-29 markets down the middle of the main thoroughfare, which was decorated with brightly coloured succulents.

Savannah stopped and nudged me. I followed her gaze to a tree, branches spread like arms, older than time, a real tree. They must have moved it sub-surface and built a crystal dome over its crown, where it poked above ground level. I had a flashback to a childhood picnic under the shade of an oak-tree, rubbing the red-gingham table-cloth between my finger and thumb, the texture of summer. I wanted to dwell in that memory, forever.

"Snap out of it," Savvie said under her breath.

We had checked the bootleg blueprints to plan this excursion, but it's one thing having a map in your head, and quite another following it with sunlight and a goddam tree filling your head with locked-away memories.

"This is it," Savannah said, pointing at the inspection hatch. She inserted the crypto-key and twisted.

"Over to you," she said with a tone that told me not to mess up, after the produce we'd traded for that cybertech.

I'd memorised the code. Twenty digits long. We'd probably get three attempts, but I didn't want a yellow light flashing on the gatehouse dashboard. There was a beep, a green flicker, and the centre coil of the hatch popped out to reveal the handle. Savvie was smiling like a kid. I pulled the handle, and the ladder slid down.

"Ladies first," I said.

When we emerged into the residence grounds, my nerves were on fire. Everything was calm, but this was unknown territory. Theoretically, there was nobody onsite. That was the intel. Didn't mean they didn't have private security, laser-trips, thermals, drones, or another defence system. We weren't exactly experts, although it wasn't our first rodeo, either.

There were panels across the surface-level ceiling, thick reinforced-acrylic, separated by joists, that made the roof a chessboard of white squares thirty foot above us. I hadn't seen this much natural light in years. The living quarters were four hundred yards away, and the grounds were like a country garden. I saw grass — real not astro — and manicured hedges. There was an orchard, densely packed with apples and pears, plus a pond with Koi carp. Damn, do these people know what it's like below? Have they seen the malnutrition, eczema, asthma, the grind for survival? They have friggin' ornamental fish basking in natural sunlight. I shook with anger.

"You know what we're here for," Savvie said. "Nothing more, let's go."

Savannah had a list of herbs for us to gather. She'd given me a chart of the simpler ones that weren't in the patch she was raiding; chewable fibre from specific roots, dock leaves, Thai-Basil, a smorgasbord of weird stuff to identify. I was on security too, keeping an eye on anything that moved, which wasn't us. Who says men can't multi-task?

I thought I might look for the items around the orchard and maybe gather a windfall or two. I was thinking apple, but then I saw it, like a perfect setting sun in miniature, an orange. The tree was festooned. Unable to resist the temptation, I pulled and twisted one, and the branch sprang up with a rustle of leaves. The scent was to die for.

"What the hell are you playing at?"

I nearly decked Savannah, who had crept up on me. "You're making more noise than a turbine at full rotation."

I tossed her a couple of segments. "Taste that," I said.

She was about to give me some grief but saw the juice dripping off my fingers and the aroma was overwhelming. She popped a slice in her mouth, face like murder, and bit down. Her eyes lit up, then half closed. Savannah's mouth stopped chewing, as she savoured it. When her eyes opened again, they were bright and she smiled, as a bead of juice dribbled over her lip, before she wiped it and giggled. I've loved her since we were fourteen. These days, I sometimes forget, who we are, who we were.

"Take three," she said.

"I can carry more."

"One each, one to trade. Any more is trouble," she stated.

Reluctantly, I did as I was told. Well, three or six, it's pretty much the same thing. Never was much good at math.

***

Every excursion was an adrenalin kick. We never took too much that it would be noticed. We didn't take chances, until the seventh trip, which must have been twenty cycles after the first excursion. Savannah had found a new place to raid, with some different items she wanted.

I'm going to call this flavour Taglia," she said.

"Like, cut?" I asked.

"It's a play on the last six letters of Nostalgia, and it means cut in Italian. You can also translate it as a reward, but I was thinking more of your clothing size, cut of the cloth."

"A reward, like a price on your head? What does it do?" I said.

Savannah looked wistful, "Remember that tee-shirt I had with the fox?"

I thought for a moment, "Yeh, like a collage, from tattered red and orange cloth? You wore it to death."

"I looovvveeed that shirt. When I see an old image of

myself wearing that, I yearn for it, even though I'd forgotten it existed. That's the Taglia sensation."

"A desire for old clothes?" I laughed.

She kidney punched me. "The memory of things you loved, that you've now lost, dopehead."

We followed the same time, same route, same process. You might say a repeatable pattern is poor strategy. We saw it as a winning formula and since it was working, why change? Anyhow, it was the bird that started the problem, and the fact that we were ten minutes late — a diversion around a security patrol that we didn't fancy encountering. Finally, we were inside. Savannah sent me off to these rows of corn, nearly shoulder high. She wanted a dandelion, thought there might be some in the weeds, since the area looked wild. The corn rows were eighty yards long, and ten rows wide. I didn't need a chart for a dandelion, I knew exactly what the yellow lion-heads looked like. A lifetime ago, I picked one and stuck it behind Savvie's ear. Thought she would knock it out, but she gave me a peck on the cheek instead. First kiss.

I saw a movement and froze, pulled back from my memory into the job. Nothing. I edged forwards, and then the blurred movement and shrieking alarm happened at once. My brain was overloaded. It's a good thing we never carry weapons, because I'd have started shooting. Then I realised it was a bird.

Savannah arrived.

"What..." was all she said, before the alarm repeated.

"Pheasant," I said.

"Shut it up, before the whole neighbourhood arrives."

There were gaps in the corn, every fifteen yards. I slipped quietly through one to find the bird. No movement. I waited and fantasised about no tofein for a few days. Pheasant breast, tender, lean meat. Pheasant stew, dripping with delicious taste. My mouth began to salivate. I saw a head jerk, a gold and black eye staring at me out of blood red feathers.

"Supper time..." I murmured enticingly, "...coo-coo-coo."

It tilted the dazzling blue and red head, as I edged closer. Suddenly, deciding I was a threat, it shot away, racing to slip through the corn. I dived forwards, but it was faster. It squawked the alarm, and this time, there was an answer. A second bird nudged out of the corn right beside me. I grabbed one wing as it darted to escape. There was a blur of feathers, claws, and a beak that I swear had teeth, plus a raucous sound like a dozen burglar alarms going wild after a storm. Savannah was back. She was ready to tear me a new a-hole, but when she saw the blood from my scratched face, feathers and shit all over me, she started laughing instead. I managed to wring the bird's neck. Brutal, but food is food.

"We'd better exit. Pronto?" I said.

Savvie was laughing so hard she couldn't respond, bent over with her hands on her knees. Then we were lit up. A bold orange spotlight like we'd walked on stage. Savannah dropped and rolled through the corn into the next row. Disorientated, I followed suit. The spotlight was still on us, and I nearly tripped over another pheasant.

"Wait!" she said, pointing above my head.

I raised my eyes, not sure what to expect — but certainly something weaponised. I had to use my free hand to shield my eyes. The acrylic roof was blazing. Hovering in the sky was a giant orange ball of fire.

"The sun," Savvie said. It had been so long since we'd seen it.

My muscles relaxed. I felt giddy with relief. "Feel that heat," I said.

Savvie leaned forward and kissed me, full on the lips.

"One day, we should come back here when we don't have to rush…" she said, her fingers brushing under my chin.

Maybe we lingered too long. We were already running late. We'd got into the habit of locking the access tunnel behind us, so we didn't leave any rabbit-holes for the curious to follow. Then we simply unlocked again to leave. I tapped the code out twice, perfectly. The panel glowed red.

"What's the problem?" Savvie asked.

"The code has timed out," I said.

"Try it again," she said.

I shook my head. "Two fails already. Third one will trigger an alert. Let's move to Plan B."

"Do we have one?"

"That's your domain," I said.

"Shit." She looked around and started walking towards the residence. I knew there was nobody at home, or they'd have been out already thanks to the noise.

"Can't go through, but there might be a side access. Let's try there," she pointed.

We found what we needed, a steel gate with a surprisingly old-fashioned padlock.

"If I had the clippers, I could slice that off in a flash," I told her.

"If I was carrying, I could blow it away, but we don't have either," she said.

I looked around. Nothing. Popping on my LED, I peered inside the lock mechanism. It was simple. If I had something narrow and hard, I might be able to tumble it. I looked at the bird swinging in my other hand.

"Hold this," I told Savvie and gave her the LED, positioning her hand so it was over the lock at the right angle. Then I switched my grip on the bird, to hold it by the claw instead of the neck. Halting the pendulum-swing of its body with my other hand I pushed one talon into the lock.

"You've got to be kidding. Picking a lock with a pheasant?" Savvie shook her head but kept the LED perfectly still.

It was clumsy, but good enough. I heard the click, tossed her the bird, and snapped the lock open. The lane was clear, as far as I could see.

"This one's going down as legend," Savannah said, silently closing the gate. We walked calmly towards the gatehouse. There was a gentle breeze, which should have acted as a warning.

"STOP!" a digitised-voice yelled.

We turned, a security drone gliding towards us, all carbon-fibre gun-barrels and whirring blades.

"Go," Savvie mouthed to me, and she spun like a discuss-thrower, to hurl the throttled bird into the low-flying drone. It was a direct hit, from both parties. The drone veered sideways to smash into the curved wall, rotors and feathers scraping down the metal, as Savvie crumpled to the floor. A rose-red stain flowering across her chest.

"Go," she whispered again, and her eyes closed for the last time.

***

You know the rest. I didn't leave her, but I got a lenient sentence, all things considered. The shop keeps me going. I've got enough stock for a few more months. After that, who knows? Life's hard, but that's nothing new. I replayed those excursions in my head, in my cell, and now when it's quiet here. The drops of fresh orange spilling over her lips, Savvie doubled over laughing, the sunlight giving her a halo, as it caressed our skin with its warm, once familiar touch. Then again, I'm using. Catch me un-flavoured and I might tell you Savannah was selfish, with no back-up plan. That she never really loved me. I was a tool to get her ingredients. She was a messy eater. We overheated under the radioactive ball of gas that pollutes our wasted planet. As the sun fried our brains, we made mistakes. Neither of us saw the alarm wire on the doorframe. A single point four-zero calibre round fired at close range from a DRJ-Kestrel drone, that left an exit wound bigger than a crater. Just another petty criminal snuffed out by our efficient law enforcement teams.

That's not how I see it, though, even when I'm off-cycle. I kept the dwindling stocks of pure Nostalgia for myself, at first. But in these dark days, we could all use a little more light, and I started giving it out for free, to the customer's I liked — the one's with respect, the people that kept some humility even in this hellhole.

Savvie never got to make the Taglia flavour — enhancing the memory of things you loved that you lost. Not sure I need it. My memories are sweet and sharp enough. I can even get the feeling about stuff we hadn't done yet. She got the name right, though. It cuts like a damned knife.

368 Friends

The employees have disappeared into their Christmas party, as we accelerate towards the end of 2007. We are the sole occupants of the office. Inside this room, the artificial light makes the whiteboards glow pale green. It's as though the four of us have been abandoned inside a giant egg, sealed away from friends and families. We all had a real existence once, months ago, before we began pursuing this sales deal we've now lost. In return for our total commitment, we will probably forfeit our jobs. Everybody in this room is technical, with complex tasks and defined roles to keep them busy, except for me. I'm just the sales guy. I'm only staying for the team's moral support, even when every instinct tells me to run.

    Cliff paces like a tiger while he talks on my mobile. I had to call the CEO to tell him we'd lost the deal. Then I gave the phone to Cliff and they're picking over the bones of the technical results like soothsayers, trying to divine a truth from the scattered remains. If we lived in a more civilised age, like the 1980's, we'd already be in a bar, bonding with alcohol and shared oblivion. As a sales guy, I know how to socialise in any situation. That's one of the few things I can do. In these politically-correct times we aren't allowed that release. Instead, we plan our damage limitation program. For the nth night in a row we'll work until morning and snatch a few hours nightmare-infested sleep. Tomorrow will be hard. We'll be zombies, with all motivation and dreams of success sucked out of us. Today's adrenalin will have drained away like so much mini-bar wine.

    Matt is texting or tweeting or changing the status on his Linked-In profile, or whatever social network is trendy this week. I'm on Facebook, but I don't really publish anything. I know Matt has over 200 friends on Facebook. I think I've got about ten, and they're all family members.

As I tap at my keyboard, the others assume I'm typing a carefully worded response to the prospect, instead of letting you know the truth. Perhaps they still believe that the right words can change anything, clinging to dreams like twenty-somethings, crafting desperate letters to departed lovers. Salespeople are meant to be Teflon-coated, rejection-proof and incapable of all emotions except greed and lust. We're infused with positive-energy and impossible to knock down like those little egg-shaped toys. I can't let them see a human side.

"Let's go back to the hotel," says Arun, breaking the silence.

"Yes, the wireless network is down. We can't do anything here," adds Matt.

"We can't do anything," I echo.

I will always remember this room, bathed in luminous light that seems to get greener by the minute while everyone taps helplessly at their keyboard. Worse than that, it will be impossible to forget my mental image of the client when we sat down this afternoon to discuss progress, with a sly smile spreading across his face as he mumbled platitudes. He knew and so did I. We still had to perform our dance, like chicken and fox.

Our nervous families are out there somewhere, nursing children, wrapping presents and worrying they can't afford them.

"One day, we'll laugh about all this," says Matt.

"When a freak tornado devastates the whole site," Arun replies, deadpan.

"I guess it's time to burn my lucky boxers." I say.

"Just remember to take them off first," Matt winks.

In the future, there'll be enough dazzling successes to make this seem insignificant. We'll frame a narrative structure around this point, making it the trough before the peak. We'll find a way to infer meaning from what's been a pure disaster.

"Time to smash the shell," I say, looking at the egg-like walls and partitions around us.

"Give me an iron bar and this place will be in more pieces than you can count," says Matt, swivelling to look at the array of expensive flat-screen monitors.

"Did somebody say bar? I'm up for that." Cliff chimes in.

"Let's go back to the hotel," Arun says again.

"Before we do something we'll regret," I say.

We use our security passes for nearly the last time. Tomorrow, they'll escort us off the premises after formally announcing the result. Outside the sky is black as despair. The glass building shines like ice and the air is cold enough to cut. Thin laughter carried on the wind shatters around us. Many years ago, I had a mentor, an experienced sales guy who'd learnt his craft at IBM. He gave me a comforting thought to help you through times like this. I wish I could remember what the hell it was.

***

One year later.
I'm singing at the top of my voice, a feel-good song. The radio volume is turned-up high, so I can pretend I'm in tune. Hard to believe we'd find another opportunity of this scale so close to *the disaster*. Yet here I am travelling to this obscure location again, passing the same miserable streets and dreaming of

triumph. I alter my route to make sure we don't repeat our mistakes. We're all governed by patterns and I'm breaking the old ones. Salespeople are highly superstitious. Engineers are so obsessed with logic that they miss the subtle power of folklore.

This time is different. We're winning. The scope was clearly defined in our favour, thanks to a lot of hard work on my part — although that activity is invisible to the rest of my team. Not that I'm looking for praise. I don't get paid for hardwork, only results. Matt tightly managed the Proof-of-Concept, tracking every element. After *the disaster* it took six months to get our new product working properly, ironing out the issues our competition had highlighted. We play our hand carefully, with the precision of a military campaign, and it feels wonderful.

Arun didn't make it. He came out of *the disaster* with nothing but credit for his technical work, but his passion and belief in our vision had died. Within a few months he was at an obscure start-up in San Fran, eliminating food waste with some sustainability eco-friendly thing. Cliff has fared better but doesn't come out of HQ anymore, controlling everything from the mothership. Got his fingers badly burnt last year. I don't think he'd realised how hard it is in the field. Hand-to-hand combat was never his cup of tea.

The sun is out and even the traffic jam can't blunt my optimism. Of course, our competitors are up to their usual tricks, but we're wiser. You need an enemy to motivate you, to get the best out of yourself. They got the prospect to make a reference call to *the disaster*. They primed them to look for the faults we showed last time, issues we've fixed. It's not about how good your product is but the pace at which it improves.

Not everything goes our way, there are some challenges, but we cope. We introduce our big man to their top dog. We leverage our partners, network, socialise, and advise our champions. The deal still must be closed though, and there's a wild card. A new manager has switched into the Exec Sponsor role. We get to shake his hand before our Procurement meeting. As I get closer to the industrial zone where they are based, I start to feel the nerves. This is my chance to perform, this is what I do.

I get my lucky parking spot. The omens are good. Mind you, getting any space in this car park is a stroke of good fortune. You must hope one of their arrogant VPs are still at lunch if you want a visitor's spot. Matt is waiting in Reception, tapping away at his phone.

"How many friends now?" I ask.

"Three hundred and sixty-eight."

"More than one a day. You'll have a busy year."

He tells me he's checked the proposal and the POC performance numbers for the third time. His foot is flexing up and down on the floor. I relax him with a joke.

"You know the one about the salesman who dies?"

He shakes his head.

"At the pearly gates St Peter says he's surprised to see him. Although his name is on the list, most salespeople prefer it in Hell. St Peter says the sales guy should take the elevator down, spend a day in Hell then make his choice. The sales guy reluctantly gets in the lift and when the door opens, he's astonished to be greeted by all his old sales buddies. They're delighted to see him. The Devil comes over and gives him a big cigar and they spend the day playing golf. In the evening, there's a slap-up meal and they go on to a club. Next morning, when he gets back to St Peter, the sales guy explains that he enjoyed Hell, and he'd like to go back if possible. St Peter prepares the forms, the sales guy signs and then returns to the lift. When he arrives in Hell, the Devil claps him in chains and brands him with a red-hot iron. All his sales buddies are being tortured in the fire-pits. What's this? screams the sales guy. It wasn't like this yesterday. The Devil smiles and says, *Yesterday, you were a prospect. Today you're a customer."*

Matt stands to greet the Exec Assistant. Hopefully she missed the end of that joke. She leads us to the conference room via the elevator. I would try and build some rapport but there's a different EA every time we come here. Makes you wonder why. I smile as the elevator goes up, thinking Procurement should be in the basement. Before the meeting starts, I tap on the beech table with crossed fingers. Knock on wood.

We begin by talking about kids and terrorists, anything but technology. Finally, the new manager calls us to order. He lays out the agenda and we start with creeping death, where each of us explains our background as we go around the table. I wait for my turn. While Matt runs through his bio my mind drags me back to *the disaster*. We had the better product, but we were unlucky. I know there is no such thing as luck, blah, blah, blah. Although experience tells me bad luck is real enough and loiters like teenagers at a strip mall. This is our chance to shift it down the street, let it hang around somebody else for a while. We've learnt so much this year. We also know the other side cheated. Technical sleights of hand to make their results look better. It's a shame we can't tell the prospect about that. Nobody likes a tell-tale though. Our sales pitch will be all about accentuating the positives.

On my two-hour drive this morning I had ample time to calculate the commission, which is almost enough to pay off my credit card. There's only so long I can live on my level of debt. Their Procurement guy leans forward and so do we.

"As you know we're highly price-sensitive."

That's good. We're significantly cheaper than our competition.

"For whatever reason," he says, "...you were late into the bidding process."

That's a lie. I don't interrupt though.

"I told you our expectation was free, and your competitor practically met that. You guys were just not there. Six-fifty capex and one-seventy kay opex," he shuts the proposal with a flurry. "Out of the ballpark."

The project manager adds with a conciliatory gesture, "It's a fast-moving space. Let's talk again in a year."

The walls seem to be curving in. Matt flaps his arms like a deranged chicken. I ask how, why, where, who, when. Open questions to probe their solid defences. I feel sick. Even while asking questions, I'm mentally rehearsing the conversation with the CEO and my wife. I can't decide which is worse. Soon afterwards they lead us out of the building. Probably a good thing since we're still dazed. Our champion stays for a moment to apologise. He did his best, he tells us. Even he is embarrassed. We shake hands and smile.

Matt and I say nothing at first. Walls have ears, and frequently cameras too. We stop by our cars, a good distance from the building. Then he says,

"Guess you should throw out your rabbit's foot."

I laugh, and he lights a cigarette.

"368 friends," I say. "How many would come to your funeral?"

"I think it's just us," he makes a wide gesture with his arm, trailing smoke.

Standing on the car park's edge we stare over the fence at the headquarters of a global distributor. They're a major name, probably Fortune 500 but they've not been on our target list. The building is palatial; its jagged skyline highlighted in golden light from the evening sun, making it shine like a crown. It's beautiful. One of the rays of light sprays out to spotlight us for a few moments. The light is warm and comforting, a positive omen. We gaze at the building and contemplate our uncertain future.

"Third time lucky?" I say.

The King's Men Vigilantes

The police advised everyone to avoid the woods, but that's like an invitation, isn't it? I couldn't persuade the rest of our shift to join us, though. They were too scared, caught up in silly superstitions. Not many people want to venture into Whitare woods on a normal Saturday night, but especially not now, when there's a nutter about.

"Are we vigilantes?" Scott asks.

"Yep," Dex says.

"Officially, we're part of the Shelley Neighbourhood Watch Scheme," I say.

Scott switches the torch on and swings the beam around experimentally, but it's not dark enough for it yet.

"What shall we call ourselves?" Dex asks.

"The Panthers?" Scott says.

"Sounds like a Football team. What about the King's Men?" Dex counters.

I toss a stone into the bushes. "I'm not sure we want to be vigilantes."

The others look at me like I'm crazy.

"Vigilantes take the law into their own hands. If vigilantes catch the weirdo they might beat the shit out of him, or string him high from that oak," I gesture.

"What's wrong with that?" Scott says.

"You're assuming it's a man?" Dex adds, with his thick local burr.

I laugh, "How many women would dress as a sadistic clown to scare people?"

Dex shakes his head in apparent disbelief at my stupidity.

"The King's Men," Scott says, defusing the situation. "I

like that."

Nobody has mentioned a destination, but we're being pulled towards the Stone as if it were a magnet. The Stone sits on the hilltop, with a panoramic view for miles. As kids, Scott and I used to climb the Stone and sit there, gazing at the chequered fields that made up our world. These days, it's encircled by a small iron fence, and a warning sign that forbids touching, advising that the Council will prosecute any offenders. I'm not sure who let them take ownership of our Stone. Anyway, if I were a crazy killer-clown, the Stone is where I'd hang-out.

"Look at this bad boy," Scott says.

He points at a huge snail climbing a fence post. He flicks the torch on to illuminate the shell, and the snail's antennae withdraw as though the light were fire.

"What a whopper," says Dex, studying it carefully. "Wish I had some salt."

"That's for slugs," I say.

"A snail's only a slug with a shell," Dex says.

"That's like saying Jenny Widdup is just a boy with tits," I tell him.

"I think you'll find there's a couple of other differences between boys and girls," Dex winks at Scott.

The snail's antennae slowly telescope back out, the right one moving faster than the left.

"We used to toss them into the sea," Scott says.

Dex has his face by the snail, inspecting it like a car engine.

Scott continues, "We'd see who could throw them furthest. They're the wrong shape for skimming."

"Let's go," I say, shoving Scott in the back, who's easy to shift, and slapping Dex to nudge him towards the steep slope leading to the crest. "Didn't know I was with two serial snail-killers."

Our breathing punctuates the air as we lean into the hill. I try to remember if antennae is the right word, of if snails possess eye stalks or tentacles. Perhaps there's a special snail-word. I could ask Dex, our self-appointed expert who freely doles out advice on all topics, but I'm not convinced science is his speciality.

"Did the saltwater kill the snails?" Dex asks Scott.

"Well, none of them swam back to shore," Scott laughs.

"Did they melt?" Dex persists.

"I think they drowned."

The incline reduces, and we pause near the crest. The sun is low, and at this angle the Stone is hidden. The top of the hill is quartered, with the Stone in the centre. The left two quadrants are thick with scrub and trees, corralled behind barbed wire as though they might escape. That area is a labyrinth of animal trails, abandoned to kids, and teenagers holding illicit meetings. On the other side, the nearest quadrant has a scattering of gorse that gradually opens to a field sweeping down the hill towards Brough Road, a mile away. It's similar on the far side, except for a group of twenty loosely clustered trees standing beyond the crown, a respectful distance from the Stone. There's a thirty-yard gap clear of bushes between the two right hand quadrants, that slopes downhill with three natural steps which alter the gradient from severe, to steep, to gentle. That's where everyone goes sledging in winter.

"What's the plan if we find the clown?" Scott asks.

Dex nods in my direction, "He can run to the Neighbourhood Watch and fill in a form," he says. "While we kick the crap outta him. Or her."

"Perfect," Scott says.

"Should I bring you back some salt?" I say, sarcastically.

Scott puts a finger to his lips. Edging over the crest, we crouch. Scott takes the lead, and moves along the gorse, so we get a view of the whole area and stay hidden. Nobody is there, apart from the Stone. Not sure what I was expecting. A circus of cavorting clowns? Jenny Widdup with a pentacle daubed on her bare skin?

Scott gestures along one side of the dark hedge-line and points to Dex and me, indicating our route. I think his plan is for us to flush out any lurkers, while he waits in ambush. He's watched too many war films, with his ridiculous commando-signals, and not enough horror — never split up, that's the golden rule.

Dex sets off, stooped low, and Scott does the same in the opposite direction. I should have said something, but nobody listens to me, so I follow Dex.

"How do they breathe?" I say, as I pull alongside him in a sandy dip.

"Who?" Dex whispers.

"Snails. Do they have lungs, or take oxygen through osmosis, like toads?"

"Does it matter?"

"They might not drown. They might be able to breathe under water."

Dex strains his neck to scan the horizon. I think for a moment he might have seen a clown, but I realise he's trying to locate Scott. An orange sunbeam hits the peak, and the Stone is spot lit, casting a shadow in our direction like a giant sundial. The light makes the Stone glow, as if the rock were translucent.

"King Eardwulf," Dex murmurs, referring to the legend.

"I wonder who put it there, and why?" I ask.

"It was the old woman. He should have run her through with his —"

"She was a witch, not some old woman," I correct him.

Dex laughs. "Same thing," then grins. "Let's have some fun with Scott."

That sounds like a bad idea. I should say no, but experience tells me Dex will trample over my objections.

"Here's what we do," he says.

***

Scott sits hidden in the undergrowth, watching shadows twist across the hill. There's a solid wall of blackthorn to his right, hawthorn on the left, and a narrow path behind. He focuses on the scene in front, where the sun has formed a pool of orange light that flows gently towards the Stone. There was a jester in the old legend, he remembers, who threatened to roast the witch, claiming she was no more useful than a bag of sticks. Scott tries to recall what happened to the witch after she turned the King into rock, and what became of the jester, but the story has faded into his childhood. A bird, or possibly a rabbit, disturbs the leaves behind him.

Rolling up his jean leg, Scott unclips his knife and feels the weight in his hand. It's a 1915 Imperial German S98/05 engineer's bayonet, a Duisberg. He passes a finger along the blade, where the original sawtooth has been ground off. Even toothless, it would be no laughing matter for any clown it encountered. To get this treasure, he'd traded a couple of WWII British pig stickers, and a modern parachute regiment issue that his brother had filched.

The late sun found the Stone. The subtle play of shadow on the wind-roughened surface gave the illusion of a crowned man. Scott slipped over a low strand of barbed wire and moved closer to the King Stone, the long bayonet clasped in his right hand.

A maniacal burst of laughter from beyond the copse made Scott swivel. As if the sun had been switched off, the Stone went black, plunging the hilltop into darkness. Something shifted in the scene, a flicker of movement from the Stone.

***

Two minutes earlier
It was a simple plan. One of us would creep behind the Stone, hidden by shadow and slope. The other would sneak below the brow of the hill, past the wild hares, and create a distraction on the right. When Scott emerged to investigate, the hider would rush Scott on his blindside and take him out with a rugby tackle, giving him the fright of his life. I wanted to be the distraction, but Dex pulled rank, or at least age.

"You're quicker than me," he said. "He'd hear me wheezing at ten yards."

That was true enough. There was a good reason Dex was our five-a-side goalkeeper. Reluctantly, I submitted to his plan. Slinking to the Stone was easy, although it still made my heart pound. Now we're all separated. Easy pickings for a sadistic clown. I should have said something, but when nobody listens, why bother? I once read that disasters aren't made with one huge mistake, but a series of small, poor decisions. I bet there was someone who disagreed with all those choices too, but never said anything.

I don't dare peek around the Stone, as it's lit like a beacon. When Dex creates the distraction, it will be safe to look, as Scott will be facing the other way. The Stone feels hot.

I'm too old for magic, but there is something special about the King Stone. Everything it's seen, over hundreds of years. The secret lovers' trysts, generations of children hurling snowballs, countless storms weathered in silence, maybe a fox slipping past at dawn with a chicken swinging from its jaws. I wonder if the King would make different choices given a second chance, and how a King decides what advice to follow, when everyone is trying to influence him. I wonder if being trapped here was a curse, or a blessing.

I hear the crazed-laugh. Even though I know it's Dex, my heart stops for a beat. The light has vanished, suddenly, and I spin around the rock to see Scott's silhouette against the menacing sky. He's looking in the wrong direction as I tear towards him, and I dive forward, targeting his soft midriff. Given my pace and gravitational advantage, I expect to blast him backwards down the grass bank. The moment before I hit, something flashes, like a star, a jewel, or the tip of a blade.

We tumble down the hill, the impact smashing all air from my lungs. I slide to a halt on the damp grass, my head lower than my feet. Everything hurts. Scott's a few feet away, his head at my chest height, and feet angled to one side. He swears. Dex jogs towards us, wheezing, and shuffling with his odd way of running.

"Gotya!" he laughs, in his high-pitched chuckle.

I try to sit but it hurts. Dex flips the switch on his torch, and we need it now. He shines it on Scott's face.

"All the gods," Dex says, and the change of tone in his voice scares me.

He shines the torch on the grass between us. It's red and slick with blood. I look at my jacket, and there's a patch of wet. Gingerly, I dab at the spot with one hand, while Dex points the torch. The blood wipes away, and Scott groans again. Dex swings the torchlight to Scott and there's a knife stuck into his thigh, with an inch of blade poking out.

"What the..." Dex keeps the beam on the knife. Scott's hands appear in the spotlight, circling the wound. I push on to my hands and knees, checking every bump and future bruise, even as my eyes stay fixed on Scott's leg and the knife.

"It's my bayonet," Scott says. "I thought I saw something, by the King."

"I told you guys, no weapons..." I say.

"Can you walk?" Dex asks. Scott shakes his head.

"Should we pull it out?" I suggest.

"No!" Scott yells.

Dex pulls me to my feet and murmurs under his breath, *he's going into shock.*

I take my iPhone out of a pocket, relieved to see the screen is still in one piece. "Hey Siri," I say. "Should I pull a knife out of a leg wound?"

There's a long pause, and it becomes obvious I have no reception. Dex checks his phone too, but we're on the same network.

"We'll carry you home," Dex decides. He grabs Scott under the arms and indicates I should take the feet. When I grasp his ankles, Scott emits a burst of profanity, but doesn't fight us, so we stagger towards the Stone. We nearly drop him at the top, because we're knackered.

"Too many friggin' burgers," Dex says.

I think he means Scott, but it could easily be a reference to his own physique and lifestyle choices.

"We're never gonna make it down the hill," I say. "One of us should get help, while the other stays with him."

"You get the help. I'll wait here," Dex says.

"I'm not dead yet," Scott comments, but doesn't give us any other hints on what to do.

As the oldest by at least a couple of decades, Dex is our

unspoken leader. He's the most experienced, he's done things I haven't even imagined, like two divorces. We all do the same role, but he's the shift leader. Sometimes though, I wonder why we listen to his advice, when he seems to have made such a mess of things.

"Chop, chop," he says. I know there's little point in arguing.

"No," I tell him, surprising myself.

Despite his permanent smile, high-pitched laugh and easy-going attitude, he can switch on an evil stare. I endure the full power of it now. He locks his eyes on mine.

"They live in the pond," Scott says softly.

I look at him lying there and consider if he's turning delirious.

"Who does, Scott?" I ask.

"Snails. They can survive in water."

"That's fresh water," Dex says and shakes his head. He turns, and shielding his body from the strengthening wind, lights a cigarette.

"Give me your jacket," I say to Dex.

Meekly, he hands the cigarette to Scott, peels the jacket off, and lays it over him, then looks down at Scott for a moment.

"Try not to bleed on it," he says.

"Tell them to bring the ambulance there," I point to the main road.

He shrugs, and without another word, saunters off towards the estate.

"Be quick!" I shout after him.

He lifts a two-fingered salute over his shoulder and disappears down the slope.

"Thanks, by the way," I say to Scott.

"For not gutting you?"

"Yep."

"Did you know it was me?" I ask him, but he doesn't reply.

We sit there for a minute, lost in silence.

"What happened to the witch," Scott says.

I pause. "Didn't she turn into a white hare — what was that phrase? *She zig-zagged over the hill and was gone.*"

"And the clown?" Scott asks.

"You mean the jester?" I correct him.

"Same thing," he says.

I shake my head. It feels cold and exposed on the hill.

Scott sucks in a breath, "Who comes up with this shit?"

There's something in his voice though, a trace of fear. Unless it's the pain.

"If you lean on me, do you think you could hop downhill?" I ask Scott.

"I can try. Shouldn't we wait for Dex and the cavalry?"

"Let's meet them halfway," I say.

The first portion down the steep part of the slope is tricky. We take a long time. Once we get into a rhythm, we start to do better, and Scott grits his teeth before each swinging step. At the corner of the field I prop him against a fence-post while I pick at the rope-knot looped around the gate's latch.

Scott sticks both hands into his pockets to keep warm, shivering badly. Then he begins to swear, quietly and repeatedly. I turn. He holds out a bedraggled, shapeless bunch of fur and skin and waits for a reaction. My brain pieces the puzzle together. It's a mask, a grubby clown mask. Scott looks at the pocket of the coat he's wearing, pulling my eyes to it. The coat that Dex left him.

I touch the mask with one finger and thumb and rub them together. It feels like old leather, a rabbit skin, or a hare.

At the bottom of the next field, I see flashing hazard lights.

"Is that the ambulance?" Scott says.

"No, it's his car."

Between the strobing lights, I make out the broad figure of Dex shuffling up the hill towards us. He's carrying something, maybe the poles of a rolled-up stretcher, or is that a shovel?

"Put it back in his pocket," I say.

Scott looks me in the eye, and I'm not sure who's the most frightened. For once though, he takes my advice. He says, "If you need my bayonet, take it."

"Do you know any good jokes?" I say.

"I'm not the jester in this pack," he tells me.

Dex is closer, his shambling figure getting bigger with each step.

"Knock, knock," I whisper.

"Who's there?"

"Cash."

Scott gulps. "Cash who?"

"Yep, we've got a real nut coming."

It's not that funny, but Scott laughs. I knock on wood.

The Twaddlers Of Newport Beach

Aleisha had thought of the perfect words to cut Stevie down to size, but now they were gone — slipped away like a seal into the bay. Waiting in line, her mind scrambled to pull them back. Aleisha placed the bottle of kettle vodka and a skinny can of pineapple flavoured RockGod on the rubberised conveyer belt. Reaching into a jar she grabbed a handful of shugga-bubba.

"These too," she said.

The cashier slowly counted them and confirmed there were ten bubblegum, as though that might be an issue, or perhaps because she understood the intended use and wanted to let her know that she knew, to make some kind of moral judgement.

"How many psychologists does it take to change a lightbulb?" Aleisha asked, more to herself than the cashier.

"Sorry?"

"Only one," she said, "but it has to want to change."

The cashier didn't laugh or react at all. She scanned one of the bubblegum and tapped the digits 1 and 0 into the till. Despite what the cashier or Stevie thought, Aleisha had no intention of changing. She tried again to remember the sharp words she'd found and lost, to defend herself in the approaching confrontation. Stevie was a few minutes away, and she would have to be armed with whatever words she could muster between here and there.

Tourist cars fumbled through the four-way stop as Aleisha crossed boldly, staying on the street to bypass a cluster of sparkly tweenies clogging the sidewalk. Boutique shops and tiny art galleries trailed in her wake as she mentally prepared her defence. Aleisha knew the high ground was lost, and it was too late for denial, but why should she justify her lifestyle at all? It wasn't like he was a saint, and yet Stevie would stand over her with folded arms and a look of disgust, or even worse, dis-interest. What friggin' century did he think this was? *Read the hashtags*, that's what she should tell him. *I'm not a victim.* It was her life, and she could do whatever the frack she wanted with it — even if, sometimes, she wasn't exactly sure what that meant.

At the end of Marine Avenue, she turned right and walked along the promenade towards the ferry, a narrow strip of beach on her left and Balboa's finest yachts jostling in the sun. Coming towards her was a girl in white shorts and a faded Tilly top, with huge sunglasses and a gigantic phone clasped sideways to her ear like a peculiar square seashell.

"I told him," she was saying, "...he's harpin', right?"

Aleisha raised a hand in a flat wave as though she were a queen and then extended it for a possible passing high five, but the girl pulled the phone away from her ear and mouthed *Wait*, holding up her palm in a halt command. She carried on her conversation for another minute, without appearing to make any effort to finish. Aleisha let her gaze wander. A towering sand sculpture modelled on something from Anaheim was being admired by kids, and one of them was drawing Tinker Bell in the wet sand. The sculptor was nowhere to be seen, but Aleisha could guess who'd made it all the same. Everyone knew everyone in a community this small.

"Aleisha!" the phone girl hugged her and then checked to confirm the call had been terminated. Or maybe she was reading a txt.

"Where's the party?" phone-girl asked, seeing the

kettle vodka poking out of the brown bag.

"I'm meant to be at Xavier's later," Aleisha said.

"Huntington Xavier or Seadrive Xavier?" the other girl asked. Aleisha paused to think about that, since she didn't know there were two. Obviously, she didn't know everyone, and she wondered what else might have changed.

"Seadrive," she said.

"He's the best. Anyway, where've you been girl? We missed ya!"

Two weeks in Vegas, and a couple of weeks out of circulation with that bug. It felt like a lifetime since Aleisha had seen anyone local.

"Busy," she lied. Her friend raised an eyebrow, but Aleisha shrugged off the unspoken question. "What did I miss?" she asked, shifting the focus back to phone-girl.

"Well, I have to tell you about Henders. Remember the guy I saw on the pier? I-saw-him-again. He was drinking a Cola Triple-Zee, which is the lowest calorie naturally sweetened drink that is more than a drink. The combined benefits of the paleogreens, whey-cool protein, and CLA for lean fat-burning have been shown to trigger an afterburner effect in men and women following an intensive-burst training program. So, I was at Fashion-Eye, when he…"

"Whoa!" Aleisha said. "What was that?"

Phone-girl looked around as though there was something to be seen, like a celebrity, or a shark chewing on a surfer.

"Cola Triple-Zee?" Aleisha said.

"That's my twaddle. Want in? I know a guy in Aliso looking for more twaddlers in our demo-gee."

Aleisha's expression asked the question.

"Yea! You've been out of the loop, girl. Everyone's twaddling now. Fifty bucks for five a day. It's quick to learn, and you keep the same line for a week."

Aleisha looked at the sunglasses facing her. She could see the sandcastle reflected, bent over by the optics so it seemed to be toppling.

"They don't pay much," was all she could think to say. Newport was getting more expensive all the time. Every girl needed a second income.

"It's fun," phone-girl said.

"You just do it when you want to?"

"Aww no, they ping me. You know the phwing! sound when we first met? That was it. Time for one of my five-a-day!" She held out the phone to illustrate the point, with a message showing. The clock said six-oh-three.

"Is that the time? I'm late."

Phone-girl hugged Aleisha again. "Stevie can wait," she said.

As Aleisha walked faster towards the ferry she wondered if the phwing! had been set to alert at a random time, or if it was carefully programmed. More worryingly, she considered whether the advert had been launched because of her presence. She wondered if she would like Cola Triple Zee and tried to remember the benefits. Was it a protein shake or a diet supplement? Were they suggesting she was fat? Then she felt bad that she'd forgotten to ask her friend about the guy.

The sun was bouncing off the water and Aleisha had left her sunglasses behind, so she kept her eyes focused on the apartments. They were perfect miniature homes with each living room fully on display; a cornucopia of marble, walnut, grand pianos, silk and ebony, ornamented and embellished into grotesque baby-mansions. The windows were crammed with cuddly toys, unicorns, and giant chess pieces — or stood stark and minimal, like an architect's fantasy. Every third house possessed cigar-smoking men with tanned skin and white chest-hair, sitting on narrow porches, with wives and daughters sprawled interchangeably across sofas and sun loungers, basking in the stares of passing strangers, while sipping margaritas.

Aleisha hopped on the ferry and waited impatiently for them to cast-off. The ferry-guy came down her side, collecting tourist dollars. He winked at her and stepped past, mumbling *annual pass*. They'd been in a few classes together only two years ago, although she hardly knew him. He seemed sweet. She was tempted to give him a business card, but that would break one of the key rules she'd been taught by Mia. It was a small group that did the weekend commute to Vegas from Santa Ana, and they were tight. They didn't advertise, and they didn't look for new members. If you were lucky, they adopted you as one of the clique. Mia had taken Aleisha under her wing and shared three years' worth of hard-won advice. Who to target, who to avoid, how to keep clear of the locals and their ringmasters, which healthcare providers were the most helpful and discrete. Aleisha had been naïve, and foolish when she started. She hated to think what might have happened without Mia and her ten golden rules. Number three was *never shit in your own backyard.*

A couple of minutes was all the ferry ride took, and she focused again on the right words for Stevie. She stepped off the boat while ferry-guy was still tying the rope. Soon the gaudy lights would switch on, and Balboa would turn into its nightly fairground. The coast was more of a theme park than Vegas or Disney. She navigated the back way to the shop, where she found Stevie outside, fiddling with the chain on an upside-down bike. He was covered in oil, as usual.

"Hey," she said, "long time."

"Hey, I won't hug you," he began with his greased arms held wide as explanation, and then stopped, caught by the double meaning in his phrase.

"We should talk," she said. "Can we go inside?"

"Sure," he gestured for her to go first, and she heard him turn the bike right way up. Glancing back, she saw Stevie grab a rag and rub his hands on it as he followed her through the open door.

"You know Lily-Ann, and this is Luis," he nodded at the couple standing by the tiny desk with its old-fashioned cash register. The room was cramped with returned day-bikes, mainly cruisers and tandems. Even the wall was suffocated with post-it notes and memos covering every inch that didn't show a faded Billabong or RipCurl poster. With an unexpected audience, her latest words disintegrated, and she stood mute.

Luis glanced at her brown bag and turned to address his question to Stevie. "You guys off to Xavier's tonight?"

"Meant to be, but I'm whacked. Might skip this one," Stevie said.

"We can give you a free ride if you want? It's no problem." Luis flicked his gaze between the two of them, sensing an issue. A tell-tale phwing! broke the awkward pause.

"Oh man," Luis said, then breathing in deeply he rattled off his line at high speed. "Auto-mate is the new way to meet professionals in Orange County. With sophisticated AI algorithms that look at public sensor data, social media postings and profiles, Amazon purchases and Goodread recommendations, they can find you the right person. No more filtering out the photoshop fakes. No more tindr-finger, or wondering if that description is too good to be true. They use big data to reveal the truth and find your ideal match. The Internet of Things is now the Internet of People. Nobody is too busy for love, thanks to Auto-mate."

Stevie was looking at the floor, but Aleisha glared at Luis.

Lily-Ann broke the awkward silence. "Yo! Rough-one this week, Luis. You are going to be mister-popular," she shook her head, and taking Luis by the elbow she led him away. "If you need a ride, call," she added, as they vanished into the evening sunlight.

Stevie headed towards the tiny closet to get clean and Aleisha hovered outside watching him repeatedly wash and re-lather his hands with some heavy-duty purple gel.

"Those marketing-things are a friggin' virus," Stevie shouted to her. "I can't wait for the fad to fade. They pay shit. People only do it to for the attention."

"I got you something," she said, and delved into the bag, pulling out the RockGod drink.

"Thanks," he said, standing the can by the sink. Pulling off his tee-shirt, he scrunched it into a ball, then used it as a cloth after splashing water over his torso. He strolled out of the closet and right past her, tossing the tee-shirt into a corner. Stevie was slim and tanned, with the obligatory six-pack. He also had a scar that ran several inches down one side of his ribs, which never seemed to change colour, a pale reminder of hard times. Stevie's physique was a natural component of his lifestyle rather than a look shaped in the gym, and he seemed oblivious to the attention he received. Pulling at the straps of his old canvas backpack, he located a crushed but clean tee-shirt and pulled it over his head.

"Have you got something to say?" he asked, facing her for the first time.

"Sorry," she said. "But I'm not even sure I need to be."

"Is this an apology or not?" he said.

"Time's elastic in Vegas, you know, especially when nobody calls."

"What happens in Vegas…" he said without a hint of humour.

"I made a mistake."

"Yep," he said. "A conference, yeh?"

Normally, it was one weekend a month. This time, she'd used a two-week vacation, expecting to pull-in big money, but it hadn't gone that well. Should have stuck to Mia's rule eight — *don't become a face*. Your best approach was to seem like another tourist, but people don't stay in Vegas more than a few days. She'd taken risks, and one had backfired. The wrong guy, a misjudged comment, and word had got back to Stevie. There were no rules from Mia about what to tell your boyfriend. A lie on a lie, she thought, or she could come clean. There was nothing to be ashamed of, apart from the lie.

"Uh-huh," she said, and turned away.

***

It was a crush at Xavier's. The house was lit with hundreds of LED bulbs, but it still seemed dark. Aleisha poured the entire kettle vodka into the punch bowl, took a chocolate martini plus a corona, and headed outside. Stevie was chatting to some super-white-blonde, and Aleisha recalled Mia's favourite derogatory term for the girls here, Newport *Bleach*. She went to break them up, with Stevie's corona. Ferry-guy intercepted her on the way.

"How d'ya like it?" he asked.

"The party?" She wobbled her head in a circle.

"I meant the blonde muscling-in. Did you know Cola Triple-Zee is the lowest calorie naturally sweetened drink that is more than a drink. The com — "

She silenced him with a throat-cutting gesture. "Third time tonight."

"You must be a trendsetter," the ferry-man said. "You better drink one soon or they'll drive you nuts."

"What d'ya mean?"

He looked at the corona she was taking to Stevie. "Is that going spare?"

She handed it over, saying, "It's not as good as Cola Triple-Zee, from what I've been told."

He laughed. "If you get profiled as a trendsetter then you've an influence circle above point 85. Most people are about point 2. The super-duffo there with the skinny arms and Clark Kent glasses, he's probably point-oh-one. Anyway, if they get you drinking it, and a few other trendsetters along the coast, it'll go wildfire. Prepare to be bombarded. Then they'll pilot LA, NY city, Vegas."

"This is horrible," she winced.

"My tip is to buy one, where they can trace your purchase. Use your watch-swipe to buy it, at South Beach Plaza or somewhere. Then they'll stop hassling."

"Won't that make it worse?"

He guzzled the beer and shook his head before swallowing. "Nope. They can't make you like it. They want you to try, and then they pray to the soda gods that you love it. They won't waste money if you only buy it once."

"It's driving me crazy," she said. "You can't talk to people without being interrupted, you can't hold a conversation."

"I'm not so sure people want to talk. If they had something interesting to report they'd have put it on Bebechat." He shrugged, and the conversation died.

Aleisha squeezed her way towards the balcony. A month out of Newport and the whole community seemed to have gone mad. She thought Vegas was supposed to be the home of insanity. Stevie was no longer on the balcony, but the bleach-blonde was in residence, with an older guy slobbering over her implants. Aleisha begged a cigarette off a man with a moustache and stood looking towards the pier, assessing the damage to her relationship. It was better than she'd hoped. Stevie knew about her transgression but seemed to think it was a one-night stand.

"Trendsetter," she said aloud, and gave a dry laugh. Mia was from Rancho Santa Margarita, but there were a few other Newport Beach girls who had the same split career. It was hard to see it becoming a trend. A few days in Vegas could fund a couple of months' rent, if you had the looks and the will.

With her cigarette finished, she took out a shugga-bubba and chewed until the flavour had gone, and her breath smelt sweet. Bubblegum could overpower anything — bad breath, alcohol, vapes, or worse.

Stevie returned from the throng and slid alongside her, leaning against the balcony. She mentally totted up the evening's twaddles. She'd had three and a half Cola Triple-Zee, CosmeticEnhance, and a toofer at the new lingerie-clothing place on the Island. The fact was that her friends were the target audience for every Gen-Z marketer down the coast, and they were ramming this new approach down their throats, while they could. In her presence, Stevie had suffered two Auto-mates, a Trojan-Bareskin which had nearly got the guy decked, and a Triumph motorbike, "for the guy that needs to get away, fast". There was a definite message coming through, and she wondered if it was only her that was noticing the patterns. Uneasily, she wondered what data they were basing the recommendations on. It was simply a matter of time before Stevie put two and two together or succumbed to the brutal ad-assault.

"Hey," she said. "Are we good?"

He exhaled. "We've taken a hit," he replied, "but we're

not sinking yet."

Aleisha gazed at the pier stretching into the night. Boats were another alternative, she thought, and local. That was convenient but awkward, harder to avoid encounters with people you knew. She'd been told there was good money for the girls that went out to the super yachts, for offshore events. Although that was heavily organised, and she didn't like the idea of being part of a group. She preferred independence. There were stories too, about what happened. Offshore meant out of immediate jurisdiction, international law applies. A few rich guys, too much blow, and anything can happen. Plus, it violated at least three more of Mia's golden rules.

"You should've told me," Stevie said, his gaze fixed somewhere past her shoulder, "What you did for kicks, or money, or both."

He knew, and she felt nauseous. One more relationship gone. "Most guys don't want to know," she said.

"I'm not most guys. Look, if you need — "

Now she was angry. "— I don't need rescuing. I'm not an oppressed sex slave or a damsel in —"

He put his hand gently on her shoulder. "— to talk, I was gonna say. I just wish you'd trust me enough to be real. No judgements, just honesty."

A familiar phwing! broke the moment.

"Oh, it's mine," she said, glancing at her phone.

"Better not be friggin' Auto-mate," he said.

"LokTight's new formula sticks anything to anything. Broken china? Fixed. Wood? Easy-peasy. Metal? Mends in a flash, a few seconds work for the world's leading superglue. The new formula can even fix a broken heart. Apply to the right body parts at the right time, and she'll be stuck on you forever. LokTight, repairs everything, better than new. Even after a big mistake, or two. In Vegas. Give it a try. What have you got to lose?"

Stevie looked at her "For real?" he said, and Aleisha smiled.

He threw his head back and laughed "You got me."

"They do say something mended can be stronger than new."

There was a beat, or two, where they stood facing each other.

"Let's find out," Stevie said, taking her hand and leading her back into the depths of the party. Aleisha smiled. She might cut back her trips to Vegas, until she figured out what she really wanted. Tossing the bag of shugga-bubba in the trash, she felt lighter. LokTight wasn't the sharp line she had planned at the cashier, but it had done the trick.

"Hey, maybe you can help me triple my income?" Stevie winked.

For a moment Aleisha registered the word triple, recalling something important about that word, but let it go. Everything was evolving and she was still in control of her life, and that felt good. After this dance, she thought, maybe she'd finally try that new Cola drink.

Wild Animals

Somewhere out there is Paul Bolan, and he's promised to kill me today. It was a public declaration, in front of the entire class, before our woodwork lesson.

Nobody came near me this afternoon, as though I had a disease. Everyone knows Bolan is gonna get me. He's a wild animal. It's home-time, and the rain is gushing down like the sky has been slashed with a knife. I can walk home in twenty-eight minutes. That's my record. I can't run across the field, because it's too slippery and I'll just fall over. Plus, I'll get plastered head to toe in mud and then Mum will kill me, besides, I don't want to draw attention to myself. I need to be quick and stealthy, as I don't stand a chance in a scrap. We all saw what happened to that posh kid from Stowe who called Bolan a gorilla at the County rugby match, and he was a lot bigger than me.

Standing on the Hall threshold, I watch the rain beat its fists against the ground. It's freezing cold. I pull the hood around my head and set off across the playground. My coat's too big for me, and Mum says I'll grow into it. The hood is so deep that it leaves me looking through a tiny window into the world. Inside the coat is a sheepskin layer that unclips. I tuck my hands tight into the pockets. They have holes and I twist my fingers through the fibres of the lining. I feel some coins wrapped inside; the lining has them trapped like flies. My other hand clutches a conker and turns it over and over, squeezing it.

The rain is closer to ice than water, yet inside my hood it's tropically hot. I imagine a jungle. I pretend that I must cut a trail home and avoid the lurking beasts. As I cross the boundary from concrete playground to swamp-field, my trousers get splattered in mud. In a real jungle, leeches would attach themselves to my bare skin where my trousers are a bit too small. You should use a fingernail to remove leeches. If you use a flame like in the movies, they regurgitate their stomach contents into your blood.

Bolan isn't a gorilla. He has the size and bulk but not the nobility, and besides, everyone knows gorillas are peaceful. Bolan is more like a baboon; strong, aggressive and cocky. He's twelve, same as me, and over six-foot tall which makes him seem twice as big as anyone our age. He's not like TV bullies because they always play to a crowd. He's a loner. My dad says bullies are cowards, but Paul Bolan isn't scared of anything. He's hard and mean and not even that stupid. Bullies are meant to be thick so bright kids can outwit them. My eldest brother says Bolan won't get any bigger and I'll catch him up one day. I told him that not all creatures stop growing.

I walk around the all-weather tennis courts, and they've become a lake. Imagine if there were hippo's under the surface. They can weigh four-thousand kilograms and like Bolan the males get larger every year. Hippo's are the most dangerous mammal in Africa. I like to think I might be dangerous. I'd love to be a black jaguar, sleek and muscular, mysterious and unpredictable. That would be cool.

Bolan's last lesson on Tuesday is maths in Miss Kendrick's classroom. That's the far side of Wykham Hall, so I have a three-minute head start. Despite that, I get nervous approaching the corner of the field. The fence is crushed down and there's a narrow gap in the hedge. Everybody on my estate passes this way. This is where the foolish explorers would get ambushed by natives. I feel sick.

I take one hand out of my pocket and hold the gatepost to swing myself over the mud. Skidding through the gap, I'm sharp on my toes like a jaguar. I walk to the second gap. The hedge is winter-thin. Smoking on the other side are three figures, none of them big enough to be Bolan. I walk to the main road. My hood is damp inside with condensation. Waiting to cross, I scrape mud from my shoes on to the kerb, like a big-cat cleaning its paws.

When the traffic becomes less of a stampede I run across. Through the estate, the road sweeps in a long curve like the bank of a river. A pack of hyenas moves along the other side. Their coats have puffed shoulders and fur-trimmed hoods from which ugly faces poke out. With their slim-fit black trousers they look top-heavy. They don't laugh but have that hungry look of pack scavengers. They call to me but it's too wet for hunting. They know I'm faster than them over a short distance. I can out sprint anyone, except Bolan.

***

Three minutes and I'll be at the alley. If I see Bolan I could knock on a door. Mum says I should ask a grown-up for help if there's trouble. I did that once when two boys followed me. A man answered.

"Can you help? They're going to beat me up." That's what I said. I felt stupid, but guessed it was better than a kicking.

"I don't want to get involved," he said and shut the door.

I can see the alley. I'm walking fast and with my head start, I think I've beaten Bolan. Although he might have left early. The teachers let him do whatever he wants. It's almost as though they're scared of him, which is silly.

The alley dips in the middle like a rope-bridge

spanning a chasm. I walk across gingerly. They paint this alley with creosote in May and it smells of blue skies. My heart is drumming. The rain has soaked through the shoulders of my coat and run down my sleeves. My pockets are soggy. I squeeze the conker in my fist as hard as I can.

Stepping on to the street I let myself breathe again. The roads are empty except for occasional cars, gliding past like riverboats. My cul-de-sac is close. After passing Ravensmead, I round the corner of Pipers Croft and head for home.

That's when I see him. Bolan. Standing on my doorstep, waiting to rip my arms out of their sockets. My brothers won't be back for another hour and my parents, even later. I flip over the fence into the old Mayor's place, then into the Runkley's. I run across their lawn crouched and grab the fence into my garden. I climb awkwardly to the higher panel and drag myself on to the garage roof. Bolan is scrambling behind me. I dash to the front where the roof becomes a porch below my bedroom. I always keep my window open. I can pull myself in and lock it shut.

The window is closed. Mum must have locked it because of the rain. Bolan has pulled himself on to the roof and is kneeling a few feet away from me. His baboon-eyes are small. He stands up. I have nowhere to run, and he knows it.

"Going somewhere?" he asks.

"I didn't mean it," I say, an apology for the thing he thinks I've said which I didn't ever say.

I grab a handful of roof chippings and hurl them, with no effect. He moves towards me, and I take a step closer to the edge. The rain is relentless but I pull-off my hood.

Diamonds are made with thousands of tonnes of pressure. They're the hardest things on the planet. You sometimes find them in the heart of a jungle. I've squeezed this conker so much that it might be a diamond now. I give it one last squeeze until my arm throbs. If I'm lucky, I'll catch him in the eye.

"Keep back!" I shout and pull my arm back. He swaggers forward, then pauses. For a moment, he senses I might be dangerous. When he moves again, I throw the conker-diamond. I hurl it with enough power and speed to go through his primate-head.

Bolan ducks.

"Is that all you've got?" he says and makes a fist.

I'm shaking. He steps close enough to hit me.

The jaguar keeps its claws sheathed until required. I pull the Stanley Knife I nicked from woodwork class out of my other sleeve and slash at Bolan. He jumps awkwardly to the side, and I lunge again before he has time to recover. I don't try to cut him because he might get mad. I want to scare him.

Bolan looks ponderous and less threatening. Now he reminds me of a rhino, clumsy, almost funny. Then I remember that rhino's are nearly as dangerous as hippo's. I slash the air again and he slips. He tries to grab the edge and flips backwards. I don't see him fall all the way, but I hear him land. There's a crack like a coconut breaking open. I peer over the roof. He stares back but doesn't move.

"Very funny Bolan," I say. "Get up."

There are some dark red splatters by his head. I hope the rain washes them away before Mum gets home. Mr. Nelson runs over from number three, shouting and squawking. He's got a big, hooked nose and the way he's circling Bolan reminds me of a vulture. I wish that Bolan would move. I hate him, but I never wanted this to happen. Mr. Nelson flaps his arms and screeches.

I don't want to be a big cat soaked in the centre of a tropical storm anymore. The sun makes everything better. I want to be a chameleon, saturated in summer heat. If I stand very still, I might blend into the wall and disappear.

I begin to wonder if Mr. Nelson saw the knife.

Bolan groans. A long, sad moan. I'm relieved he's not dead, probably just knocked out for a few seconds. I'm not sure if that's good or bad news for me. Nervously, I peer over the edge. He's sitting up and dabbing one hand gingerly at a cut on the back of his head, then staring at the blood when he brings his hand back in front of his face. I swing down off the roof, holding on to the lip with both hands, and drop the last couple of feet. Bolan jerks back when he sees me.

"What the hell were you boys doing?" Mr. Nelson says.

Before Bolan can answer, I say, "We were trying to get our football off the garage roof, and Paul slipped."

Mr. Nelson turns to look at Bolan, who thinks for a moment, weighing up his options. "That's right," he says after a heavy pause. He's considering the witnesses at school, who saw him threaten me. He's probably wondering if he'd get in more trouble for the attack, or if I'd carry the can for using a knife. Maybe he just doesn't want his parents called to the school again.

Mr. Nelson tells us to wait there, and dashes off to his house, shouting something. I'm not sure if he's getting a bandage, or calling a doctor, as his words are drowned out by the rain. Bolan stands up, with one hand still holding the back of his head. He towers over me. I stare back, not sure what he's going to do next.

"There's more to you than I thought," he says.

I shrug, wondering what's coming next.

We both hear a door slam, and glance at number three. Mr. Nelson has emerged again, this time wearing a coat that makes him look like someone from those black and white detective movies on TV, Saturday mornings.

"Thanks for covering," Bolan says.

"No problem," I say, and impulsively, offer him a handshake.

He's got blood all over his right hand. He doesn't wipe it off but reaches out slowly and deliberately to shake my hand.

"You're a wild animal," he says, and smiles.

Fragile

Alan framed them on the bridge with a ribbon of coloured houses as a backdrop. When the shutter-button was partially depressed his wife and daughter's blue eyes whirred into sharp focus, smudging the houses into a gorgeous blurred-spectrum. Alan liked the way a camera could improve the world, in small degrees.

"On a count of three, shout gelato!"

They yelled in unison and Alan waited a moment to capture the laugh. Click. A perfect memory of a delightful Easter trip. Alan couldn't help but think that it was only a high if there was a contrasting low, no peaks without troughs. Fleetingly, he thought about the glass heart they had bought in Murano, and shivered.

"Let's get a real ice cream," he said.

His daughter skipped towards the café. Alan glanced down at the camera's screen, which kept the image frozen for a few seconds and tilted it for his wife to see.

She smiled and spread her arms out in the sun. "Mmm, I adore Venice. I feel like a different person."

The lady at the café stuck a chocolate stick into his daughter's ice-cream.

"You have the hair like sun rays," the lady said.

His daughter beamed but was too shy to reply. All three of them were blonde mirror-images, drawing attention amongst the dark-haired locals. Wandering beside the canal they licked their melting treats. Alan's wife spotted a picturesque cluster of buildings and they set-off to explore. The light was warm, but there were still cold shadows. Alan's camera dangled from his wrist on a cord as they lingered on a tiny bridge and gazed downstream, basking in tiger-stripes of light.

"Un foto?"

A young man faced them with a shock of black hair and a broad smile. He made a charade of crouching and snapping a photo. Alan's wife thanked the man and made the family huddle. There were hardly any pictures of them all together. Alan showed the man which button to press.

"Cheeeese," the man said in his Italian accent, and the shutter clicked.

Alan licked a drip off his cone that had been racing towards his hand while he posed for the picture.

"Hey!" His wife shouted.

Alan looked to see the youth sprinting away with their camera. Instinctively, he hurtled after him, dropping his ice-cream to splatter behind. Anger propelled him forwards. He was mad for not trusting his instincts. He should never have given the man his camera. He was mad with his wife too. Their perfect weekend was fragile, like the delicate heart of Murano glass they had chosen together and seen gently enveloped in tissue paper.

Although the man had a head start Alan was gaining ground and confidence, until the man side-stepped into a lane. Alan suddenly appreciated how hard it might be to keep sight of his target in the labyrinthine streets. He raced past a candy store, a shop of leather journals, and a gaggle of oriental tourists. He called out *thief*. Nobody reacted. He tried to recall the Italian word for thief. Ragnarok?

"Rani!" he shouted. Then he remembered that meant spider or was it a toad? The witch's familiar. Perhaps he was cursed. What was it that disturbed him so much about the glass heart the old lady had wrapped so precisely?

The thief was quick. The lanes were warped, skinny

and dark, shadows and sunlight weaving over stones to create a bewildering carpet. Alan was athletic, though, and closing in on his hare. Stamina was one of the few advantages of age. The camera was not valuable, only the memories. He mentally catalogued the stolen pictures. A holiday seized, three days of fun that were intensely more valuable now that someone had stolen them. With less than ten-yards gap, he wondered what he would do if he caught the man.

His quarry wore a loose polo shirt, jeans with a flapping belt and dirty designer trainers. He was thin but fast. Alan thought he could handle him physically, unless there was a knife. The man-boy slipped down an alley and Alan pumped his arms to make up ground. The man-boy glanced back at the echoing pursuit, eyes wide and white. Alan saw a flash of Nike swoosh and green water. The thief had jumped the canal. Alan leapt too, clearing the narrow waterway but staggering into the square beyond. A gondolier was yelling insults. The man-boy tossed the camera high in the air and Alan swerved to intercept it. The camera skidded over cobblestones towards the canal but hit a stone lip and stopped. Alan grasped it with sweating hands. A cursory inspection showed the glass screen was scratched but intact. The thief had vanished, and people were staring. Alan slipped the cord back over his wrist and held the camera tight. He was not going to jump back over the canal, where the gondolier was still pontificating. Embarrassed, he elected to follow the canal to a bridge.

The canal twisted as crazily as the lanes, and soon there was no path, and Alan was forced to veer off at a tangent. Disorientated, he wondered if he would ever retrace his route back to his past existence. Swivelling like a compass Alan moved along the heading where he felt his wife and daughter were stranded. He felt uncomfortable, and began to think it would be more accurate to say they had been abandoned.

Alan inspected each building for recognisable features, something to show he was getting closer to home. There was a mask shop. He stared at the grotesques on display. A dainty cat-mask with diamonds and huge feathers, and several harlequins glaring with menace. There was a black mask with a tiny picture of a broken heart in one corner. Alan began shaking. It was shock, he told himself. *There are many secrets to glass-blowing*, the lady in Murano had said. *You must care for this*, she'd whispered when presenting the bound heart, and had gripped his hands longer than was comfortable.

His wife would return to the hotel. They wouldn't stand on the bridge forever. If the tables were turned, he wondered how long he would wait. What was the etiquette for vanished partners? He hoped his wife hadn't called the police. All that foreign paperwork. He would erase the incident. Alan would make an album at home with his photo's, his narrative. The theft and the glass heart would be lost, like all dangerous episodes that accumulate in a relationship, shoved under carpets and behind curtains, barely showing. He wished they'd never bought the fragile heart.

There was a café. It might have a phone he could use to call the hotel. Alan pointed to a coke and the waiter gestured to a table. Alan sat and inspected the camera. Nervously, he flicked it on. The lens extended with a comforting mechanical purr. He pressed playback and the Grand Canal appeared. That was wrong. It should have shown the last image, three blonde heads on the bridge. It was two days since the Grand Canal. He flicked forwards through time, hoping the memory wasn't damaged. Different perspectives cascaded past, the ferry, Napoleon's seized house, a bronze lion. He paused on that photograph. It was pin-sharp with excellent composition. Alan couldn't recall taking the photo, but they shared the camera. It could have been his wife.

Rapidly panning through the pictures, he saw architectural angles, gondolas, magnified elements, silhouette art-shots, and finally a family picture. Wife and daughter posing with umbrellas in a thunderstorm. Except, it wasn't his family. The wife and daughter were olive-skinned brunettes, with doe-brown eyes. There was no doubt the two people were related, with such similar features. He flipped to the next picture, which was a portrait of the woman. She was beautiful and seemed familiar, like a face in a dream. He raced through the remaining pictures finding only images of the woman and daughter — together, individually, in different scenes, scattered across Venice like confetti.

The waiter placed a glass at his table with a wedge of lime and a handful of ice. Alan waited impatiently for the waiter to leave and considered how he'd been tricked. The thief had switched cameras. Was it a scam? Most likely the man-boy had been stealing cameras all day and tossed one randomly to throw him off the trail. It seemed a co-incidence that it was the right make and model. He gulped down the coke and reviewed the images again, dwelling on the woman's portrait. She seemed so familiar, like his ex-girlfriend from university. The same sheen of black hair and bewitching eyes. He didn't possess a single photo from that era. Life had been for living then, not recording. Trying to recall her face now all he could see was the camera-imposed image. With different life choices would this have been his wife? His daughter? Alan decided to return to the hotel immediately.

Although the waiter gave precise directions, Alan was lost again within minutes. The passages mirrored Alan's confusion, images and memories switching places at every twist or fork. Everywhere seemed to be a knot of floating structures or ideas held together by bridges and washing lines, bumping and scraping into new shapes and patterns. Crossing one small footbridge he saw an old-fashioned printer's shop that he remembered. Inside was a Heidelberg machine, like his father's business years before. He was sure that he could reach the hotel from this solid anchor-point. Confidently, he took the right-lane and walked to a thoroughfare lined with tourist trash. Five minutes at a determined pace and he would be at their hotel.

It was his wife that had broken the heart, the night before, accidentally swiping it off the bedside table with her handbag. He'd been irritated but had tried not to show it. This was one more small annoyance, an extra piece of accumulated damage to their relationship. The heart was broken. The blame could not be transferred though. The shop owner had made it clear that she had entrusted it to Alan. His mind wandered, considering what might have been, with different choices.

A few paces after the patisserie stood the hotel, much to his relief. At least one piece of his memory was intact. If the police were there, he would have to surrender the camera, and he felt a sting of regret. He wanted to keep the portrait of his mystery woman and possess a life that might have been. Her image was filling his head, the one that got away, the wife of his dreams, if he'd taken a different route through a chaotic life. He would quickly take the elevator to their room before his family returned and copy the woman's image to his iPad before passing the camera to the police. Nobody would know, a tiny theft. He wanted to keep his dreams alive a little longer. He knew how easily they could be broken and crushed, but he wondered if they could be pieced together differently.

"If I could make a wish…" pushing on the gilded revolving door he stepped into the hotel lobby.

His wife and daughter were at the reception counter, along with two carabinieri distinctive for their pale blue shirts and terminator-style shades. His daughter saw him first. She shouted, and his wife, the carabinieri, two receptionists and a tall man with blonde hair turned to look. Alan stared at the doppelgänger holding his wife's hand.

"That's him," his wife shrieked. "The thief!"

She pointed a finger at Alan, their wedding ring glinting like a knife. The carabinieri were on him before he could react. His mouth opened and closed but the words that fell out were foreign, strange and distorted. As the police dragged him outside, he twisted his head to see his family, but Alan succeeded only in catching his reflection in the hotel's polished glass mirrors; he saw jeans, scruffy polo shirt, dirty trainers and a shock of wild black hair.

Laughing At Funerals

The boss told us it was an easy job, but there's no such thing. We weren't born yesterday. It isn't a full removal though, only a piano. We've shifted plenty before and they're bloody heavy, and tricky too, because you can't dismantle them. At least this time there's no owner hanging around, screeching like a mynah bird at the first sign of danger. I don't like having to deal with customers, I prefer my dealings to be solid and trustworthy. An old coffer, a dresser, bookcases, chairs and tables — they all do what they're meant to and live much longer than us, serenely shifting owners with barely a murmur. Pianos are an exception, a necessary evil. This instrument looks ancient. The thing weighs a ton because it's made of real wood, not those thin planks they bang together for modern instruments. I tickle a few notes, and the boss tells me to stop messing about and get a dust sheet. I'd say the keys are real ivory. We load her up and hop in the van. Andy's driving, Neil's the navigator, while the boss and I squeeze into the middle of the van's bench seat.

"Head towards Margate," Neil says.

I suck in my breath. "Enemy territory," I say.

"Brace yourself," the boss runs a hand over his balding head. "We'll be deep in Yorkshire. Better stay silent, don't want anyone t'catch tha' Blackpool accent."

I tell them, "My grandfather was a passionate Lancastrian. Red rose to the bone."

"Wasn't he a tradesman?" the boss asks.

"Yeah, a sparky. We always knew when the Electric Board were coming. He'd rig the meter to run backwards for a few days. I remember hiding behind the sofa with my mam while the officials hammered on the door."

The boss laughs, "Cheeky blighter!"

"He was a black sheep, but fun. Could make the devil laugh, that one. Caught up with my grandfather in the end. Too many ciggies, too many bars. Cancer."

The other three nod, we've all lost someone that way.

"He stayed with my mam's twin when he got bad. She's in Yorkshire now, near Howarth. He didn't live much longer. I went to the funeral. We had one of those big black cars to follow the hearse, for the family. As we drove along my uncle suddenly turned and told me, *your grandfather always said he wouldn't be seen dead in Yorkshire.*"

Neil and Andy guffaw.

"It's true as well, my grandfather used to say those exact words. Anyway, we pull up outside the crematorium and can't stop laughing. There's the rest of the family and his friends, all waiting outside, nearest and dearest. We're staggering out of the car with tears of laughter streaming down our faces. Should've seen their looks. Nothing we could do though, it's a family curse, we always laugh at funerals."

Neil glances at the map. "You should have taken that left," he says.

Andy gives him a look, "Shall I turn?" he asks.

The road's very narrow, with a stone wall on one side and a ditch on the other. Any three-point turn is going to be tricky.

"No," Neil says, turning the map on its side. "Take the next left. I mean right."

Andy shakes his head and sighs. He slows down and keeps a look out for the next right. The boss peers out of the window, deep in thought.

"Can't afford to get lost today, lads," the boss finally says. "I want to be settled in by the goggle-box with a cold

Guinness, long before kick-off."

**

By one o'clock, we're lost. Neil tilts the map carefully as though it's one of those parlour games where you navigate a silver ball through a maze. We're looking for an isolated rural house nestled between the canal and railway. We have a photo. It feels like we're close, but there don't seem to be enough bridges. Twice, we've followed a road that parallels the railway, and then curls away to a bridge, where we loop over and find ourselves trapped by the canal.

"What next?" Andy asks.

"Does this look familiar?" Neil answers.

"Give me the damned map," the boss says.

I stare across the railway at the fields. There's a smattering of trees, an old water trough, and a house that looks a thousand years old.

"Wait!" I yell.

Andy slams on the brakes, and the back of the truck zings like a startled xylophone.

"Isn't that it?" I point to the house across the railway line.

The boss gets the photo off the dashboard. "Good man," he slaps me, playfully.

Andy pulls over. We climb out of the cabin and stretch. The house is less than fifty yards away. Unfortunately, the railway line is between us, with a steep embankment either side, as the track is thirty feet below the road's level. Andy shakes his head.

"We need a bridge," he says.

The boss glances at his watch. "We've tried that. We'll take it down and across," he says authoritatively.

Neil looks down the line, which curves so you can't see more than a quarter mile from our vantage point. "What if a train comes?"

The boss considers that. "It's probably disused. They've shut down most of these regional lines."

We all stare at the track. It doesn't look disused. There are no weeds pushing up the sleepers and the rails look polished.

The boss reads our minds. "There'll be one train an hour, worst case." Nobody moves. "Well, what are you waiting for?" He asks. "It's a fixed-price contract, you're not getting paid by the hour. Let's get lively."

Neil rigs up some ropes, while Andy and I shift the piano onto a wheelie cart. The bank looks slippery. I grip the dust sheet, more for balance than any pretence I could hold it if the ropes let out too fast. Andy's on the other side, doing the same. Neil and the boss puff as they lower it, a handful of rope at a time.

"What other funerals have you laughed at, then?" Andy asks.

"My aunt's. We're singing some hymn I've never heard. It's like guess the tune."

"Then stay silent," Andy says.

"That's exactly what I decide for the second hymn, but I mouth along so nobody can tell. I glance left, and my brother's doing the same, the two of us opening and shutting our mouths like bloody goldfish."

"That would set me off," Andy says.

"We fell apart. My stomach heaving, trying not to laugh aloud. The hardest part is after the song finishes, and we have to sit quietly through the serious parts."

"Agony," he says.

"People think the whole family's heartless because we

laugh when we should cry. Doesn't mean we're crazy, right?"

"Unless you cry when you should laugh," Andy says.

The piano lurches forward. "Woah, steady!" Andy calls.

I look left for a train. Nothing. I'm sweating buckets.

Soon, the piano rests at the bottom of the embankment. Now we need to haul it on to the other side. Neil takes the rope up the opposite bank to find something to hook it around. We watch him scrabble and slide. His feet scrape away grass to leave dark channels of mud. His knees and hands are brown when he turns around at the top.

"The rope won't stretch to the house, and there are no trees," he says.

"Let's try brute force," the boss says. He sends me to join Neil, leaving himself and Andy to push from below. They lean their backs into the piano. I'm standing behind Neil at the top of the embankment, like we're in a tug-o-war competition.

"Go!" shouts the boss.

The rope moves with surprising ease at first, and I take two paces back. Neil is straining in front of me, and my feet slide as I try to get more grip. With another xylophone-like sigh from the piano, Neil and I are dragged back to our starting position. The boss commands us to try again, with more effort, but the result is the same.

"Is this the Chorley line?" Andy asks.

He gets a mouthful from the boss. Neil and I laugh, but we're not the ones standing on the track. The boss sends me to the house to see if the owner has a car for a tow. His instructions include some direct consequences regarding my future ability to father children, if I don't act quickly.

I sprint to the building, vault over a wall, and look for signs of life. The place looks closed. There are no cars in the driveway, although there are plenty of outhouses where you could store a vehicle. I bang three times on the door with my fist. Silence. I'm about to turn back when I hear the bolts being thrown open. The door swings and an older man stands there with a mop of silver hair, although he still has a slim and athletic build.

"Let me guess," he says, holding up a finger. He cocks his head to one side and says, "You've come about the piano, haven't you Paul?"

"Do I know you?" I ask.

"I know your grandfather. Fine pianist."

I should tell him that he's dead, but it's awkward, and besides, I don't have time.

"Self-taught," I say, proudly. "Never had a single lesson but can play anything."

The man smiles warmly, "I've seen him perform in bars, for drinks and tips. The life and soul..." he snaps out of his reverie. "You must think I'm terribly rude," he says, "Come inside."

"Actually, I came for help. Do you own a car with a tow hook?"

He looks at me quizzically, and I ramble. "The piano, your piano, is stuck on the railway line, sorry about that, we got into a little trouble with the navigation, and anyway, long story short, we need to pull it out. Do you have a car? Or a tractor?" I pause for a moment, not quite sure how he's going to react. As I said, I'm not so good with customers. When he doesn't respond, I add, "We have our own rope."

"That might come in handy," he says dryly, and steps inside the house, leaving the door wide open. I'm not sure if I'm meant to follow. The house is black inside, and I can't see a thing.

"Hello?" I call.

"Come in," he shouts.

I scrape my muddy feet on the mat, and step inside. There's a dim glow ahead and I follow it, groping my way down the hall, smacking my head hard on a low beam that I didn't see. It throbs, and I know I'll have a huge egg there later.

"Watch out for the beam," he calls.

I wobble into the kitchen, rubbing my head, feeling dizzy. It's hot, and there's a muscular wood-burning stove crouched in one corner. The man sits at a table where a tiny stub of candle is lit. He gestures for me to sit down, and sensing my hesitation, tells me there's only one train per day.

"Do you know what this is?" He nods at the long yellow flame.

I shake my head.

"It's an inch of candle. An auction. You place bids, and counter bids, until the candle goes out. Last bid wins. Very traditional, but out of fashion these days."

"We need to get something to pull the piano," I say, not sure what's happening.

"Precisely. I can do that, but what are you going to bid for my help?"

"It's your piano, isn't it? Don't you want it saved?" I'm confused.

"Let's say you start at a farthing. Then if you win the auction, you pay me and I help rescue the piano and your friends. Does that sound fair?"

"I don't get it," I say. "Besides, you can't have an auction with only two people."

He takes a drag on his cigarette while he looks at me. Slowly he exhales, and the smoke spirals and twists. He taps his cigarette rhythmically on an ashtray. The smoke looks fragile, like caramel or strings of treacle toffee. I imagine you could snap a tiny piece off, and the rest would collapse and shatter.

"Two's company, three's a crowd," he smiles. "I'll counter-bid the tip of your little finger." He wiggles his own fingertip but looks at mine and smiles again, then feigns concern. "Unless you play the piano — you don't though, do you Paul?"

I shake my head, "What did you say your name is?"

"The candle's burning. I'd make a bid and then ask a question, if I were you. A little hint from the wise," he brushes the smoke away.

"A penny," I say.

"For my thoughts? That's underselling, don't you think? Not to sound arrogant, but really, are anyone's contemplations that worthless?"

I'm not sure what the hell this guy's doing, but I don't like it. I've had enough of his game. I stand up, and my chair scrapes in a chalk-on-blackboard way.

"I need to get back," I tell him. A part of me expects to find my feet rooted to the ground, or the door swinging shut and locking behind me. Old houses give me the creeps. I walk clumsily towards the hall.

"Of course," he says, and I stop to listen. "The candle keeps burning, and if you're not here to bid, then my next offer wins by default. Once you've started a candle auction, you can't finish until the flame is out. Those are the rules."

I should keep walking, but I don't. There's no supernatural power holding me from the door, only fear. It's a powerful force. My head throbs, and my feet itch to run.

"How about three years' bad luck?" he offers.

"That's..." I was going to say crazy, but this whole thing is mad, and instead, the word "excessive," slips out.

"Really? I thought it was rather considerate. You get seven years for breaking a common mirror, and in your line of work that must be a frequent occurrence."

People often think that, but we're careful. Things do get broken, that's inevitable. Some of the stuff we move has rotted in place for sixty years. Certain items end up like egg shells, the slightest nudge and they collapse to dust. We always take the blame. Mirrors though, we treat with care. We're hugely superstitious. We avoid walking under ladders, crossing paths with black cats, and none of us would ever challenge the devil to a game of chess. Of course, he's smart enough to trick you into playing his games.

I walk back to the table, knock on wood, and make my next bid.

"Two bob," I say. "And tell me the rules again."

"I've told you. It's simple," and for the first time I hear annoyance in his voice.

"You need to repeat them, given the stakes. Doesn't that sound fair?" I parrot his earlier words back at him.

He laughs, "Nice try. Keep me talking, eh? Let the candle burn down while your bid is on the table. It's like any other auction, Paul. Only the ending is unpredictable, a touch chaotic. Bidding starts slow, and speeds up towards the end, as people get desperate."

That's exactly what I'd realised about a minute ago. It's a sucker's game. He wins whatever happens. If we keep upping the price, before you know it I'll be waging a fortune against my soul. Even if I win, I won't be able to pay. Of course, he'll let me win. He's a con-artist, out to make money. That's what I tell myself, because I prefer that explanation to the alternative.

"Five funerals a year," he says.

"What does that mean?" I ask.

"It means you'll attend five funerals every year," he says, in a matter-of-fact way.

"Whose funerals?"

"You can't know in advance because that would spoil the fun." He stubs the cigarette out in the ashtray.

"Spoil the fun?" I say, incredulous.

"Sure. You love funerals, don't you? You're always laughing at them."

His eyes scare me. Plus, the fact that he seems to know a lot about my life. I reason, he must have heard me talking to Andy, a few minutes earlier. He's good at what he does, I'll give him that.

"It could be family, friends, lovers, neighbours, children," he says. "Or a handful of work colleagues on a railway line. People you know well enough that you'll be obliged to attend."

"Two bob and a farthing," I tell him.

"Now that's not fair, is it?" he says, fixing his stare on me.

"Why not?" Delay, delay, delay.

I see him glance at the candle. I can't remember exactly how high it was when we started, but he'd said it was an inch. Looks like half an inch left.

"The bidding should go up with incremental stages. Sixpence, Shilling, Florin, Half a Crown, a Pound," he looks offended as he explains this.

"What happened to the full crown? You can't leap from half a crown to a pound. That's not incremental. You're bending the rules in your favour. Not that it was in the rules."

Keep talking, I think, and resist the urge to glance at the candle because I don't want him doing the same. "I asked you to clarify the rules. I don't remember anything about the bidding going up in stages. You can bid anything, as long as it's an increase. If you ask me —"

"The eternal soul of your first-born child," he says, deadpan.

"Christ," I say, which might be a mistake. "Isn't that a bit clichéd?"

He shrugs. "Tradition often sounds that way. I don't normally jump ahead in the bidding, but since you're breaking our accord with your penny-pinching bids, you're giving me permission to do so as well. You see, there are unwritten rules. We'd be here all day if I had to explain those. No fighting, for example. This is a civilised auction. We should keep it that way, don't you think?"

I nod assent.

"I'm glad you agree." He launches into a monologue about the state of society and the value of manners, and I listen, drawn in by his patter and wit. I must admit he's fascinating. I'm not entirely sure what his game is, but I feel obliged to keep playing. Vaguely, I register that I haven't made another bid yet. If he is a con-artist, the best strategy would be for me to lose the auction, so I don't owe him anything. Let him win. I'm not sure I'm entirely comfortable with that approach, and I wonder if he's delusional. He's certainly mesmerising. Hypnotically, he lights another cigarette, and the smoke seems to stop and start in the air, as though there's a bubble of time which he can control at will. The smoke rolls forward and backward while his words tangle around me. Something about his gesture reminds me of my grandfather. Not sure what he did exactly that sparked that memory, if it was deliberate, or if it matters.

My grandfather was wiry-haired, with a raucous laugh. He used to smoke in the evenings, with a towering ashtray beside his chair, that would topple at the slightest nudge. I recall him sitting there, with the smell of chicken soup brewing in the pressure cooker, which was divine, and the high-pitched whistle the cooker used to make, like the sound of an approaching train. We would play cards, drink dandelion and burdock, and everybody would be laughing. Sometimes we'd sing as he played the piano. Wasn't there something important I had to do about a piano? The candle flame I'm staring at flickers. *The piano.* What could be so important about that? I let it go. I remember my grandfather's smiling face, his earthy smell as he tucked me into bed, and the coughing of an unseen lodger in the room below. Every night, my grandfather would kiss me on my forehead, turn and —

"A crown," I say, alert in the kitchen with the silver-haired man. I know what to do. I snap my arm across the table and snuff out the candle with my thumb and forefinger, like my grandfather did every night. The room goes black.

For a few moments, I daren't move. Or maybe I remain where I am for longer, I feel disorientated. My head throbs, and I rest it in my hands. The light from the stove has been extinguished, and it's bitterly cold, as though the fire has never been on. Opening my eyes, I stand and cautiously navigate my way across the kitchen, to throw open the window shutter. A welcome ray of light penetrates the darkness. I'm alone. Quickly, I head across the kitchen towards the hallway that leads outside. Then I stop and dig deep into my pockets. I pull out half a crown, two shillings and a sixpence, and go back to leave them on the table.

"There are rules," I say aloud. Good money gone to waste, is what I think, but I recall my grandfather telling me *better to be safe than sorry*.

The hall is black. I hear a whistle, a long, slow, deep blow that changes pitch. The train is arriving. I can feel it in my feet, tonnes of steel hurtling down the line, making the ground reverberate. I rush down the corridor, almost tripping as I suddenly remember to duck beneath the beam, and then burst outside. Blinded at first by the light, it takes a moment before

I can take in the scene. The smoke of the engine is pouring into the sky from the depths of the sunken embankment. It's too close and too fast. I race towards the line, shouting and screaming at everyone to run, but it's futile because I can't outpace the train. It screams past, the whistle transforming from a peep to a howl. I stop, and as the sound retreats, I hear laughter. To my side, half hidden by the wall, stand Neil, Andy, my boss and the piano.

A rope is attached to the huge instrument, and loops through to a tractor. I feel like a total idiot. One bang on the head and I go delirious. I should retrace my steps and collect my money, but I know that's not going to happen.

"Fat good you were," yells the boss over the disappearing train. "It's a good thing this gentleman came along, or the piano would be halfway to Chorley."

The silver-haired man sitting on the tractor smiles. I want to laugh, I really do.

Instead, I cry.

Butterfly

My form is completed with a neat row of checkboxes showing no disease, no early deaths in the family, no allergies, and no mental-health problems. A few white lies never hurt anybody. At least, I tell myself that. After two days of hitchhiking and sleeping under bridges I can't afford to get rejected for the wrong answer. I should also tick no money, no luck, no useful qualifications, and no way I'm going back to Berlin without this cash. They don't have checkboxes for any of those. I desperately need the nurse to say yes. I've tried everything; landscape gardener, tiler, chippy, decorator, but the work has dried up. It doesn't help that I don't speak the lingo. This cash is my lifeline.

The nurse is heavily pregnant. She flicks through my form.

"Hay-fever?" she asks and my face flushes red, like I've been caught cheating in a school exam. Not that I ever did cheat. At least, not in exams. Perhaps I should have done, then I could have gotten to university, or at least a better job — but in that case I would probably have never made it to Berlin. I guess things work out for the best in the end.

"No," I say in what I hope is a firm tone. I don't say anything else because I'm a hopeless liar. There must be something I'm good at, everyone has a talent. The nurse sighs.

Williams said it was easy money. *You'll probably be a placebo anyway*, he told me. I didn't want to come here but the maths was compelling: Monica lives in Berlin, and one week in the clinic is enough cash to stay in Berlin for three more months. Simple. That's provided Williams lets me carry on sleeping on his sofa. Without this cash, I'll be forced to use my return ticket to Sydney and leave Berlin — and more importantly Monica. I'd lose everything. Mind you, without Monica, Berlin is another dead-end. With her, and enough bought time to get a proper job — like those three months — who knows, it might become home. My friendship with Williams probably won't survive, whatever happens next. I wondered if he told me about the clinic because he thinks I won't go back to Berlin afterwards. He's always telling me I'm a drifter. Says I can't commit to anything, calls me *butterfly*. That's not true, not anymore. I'm changing. I can do anything if I'm motivated, and Monica is one helluva goal. Never really cared like this for anyone, before. I need to stay in Berlin, and I'll do whatever it takes, even be a guinea-pig for new drugs.

"Rules," the nurse says. "Number one, you stay on the facility for five days. A payment is made unless you are discharged sooner."

I'm sure that should be earlier, not sooner. Sounds like a broken grammatical rule. The Germans are confusing. If I stay here too long, I'll forget how to speak English. I've already adopted a strange accent to make it easier for people to understand me.

"Rule two. No alcohol, drugs, cigarettes or masturbation on the facility."

"Sure," I say, wondering which I would miss first.

"Rule three. All trips to the bathroom must be accompanied."

Of the four items in rule two, I wonder which they think accompanied trips will prevent, and then I hope they have male nurses. I wouldn't be keen on the pregnant nurse standing over me at a urinal.

The clinic is in the middle of a residential estate and could easily be a large house. Inside, it has the bland decoration of a hospital. The walls, ceiling and even my folded gown are beige.

The air reeks of antiseptic, sharp and clinical, masking something rotten. The nurse leads me to a shower room. It feels good to let the water and heat wash the journey away. Reluctantly, I finish and slide the shower-door open. Cold air hits me. The mirror is condensation free and I catch myself full frontal, brown eyes staring back. We only have a shaving mirror in the flat and I haven't seen myself since I left Sydney. I look different, skinnier. My ribs show and my stomach is flat from lack of food rather than prolonged exercise. The main changes aren't visible though, and they don't scrub away so easily. I towel down and wait on a hard chair in my beige robe.

The nurse returns and hands me a clipboard with several paragraphs of very small print. There's an X for my signature and another for the date. I sign with a flourish and she gestures that I should follow her.

The robe billows behind me when I walk, exposing everything to the world. The floor is hard concrete with a sheen like a fever, but cold enough to make my toes curl. I can do this for five days, whatever Williams says. I'm not a butterfly, and this is love.

There are occasional doors with temporary names handwritten on cardboard and slid into metal holders. One door is ajar, and I glimpse a dreadlocked guy with brown skin. He's reading but I can't see what the book is, although the cover looks creamy and intellectual, not some airport thriller.

Ahead of me the nurse knocks and then opens a door. I see a box room converted into a study. A man with rimless glasses stands up behind his desk. I walk over.

"I am Doctor Leiben," he says.

The Doctor has a firm handshake and equally strong accent.

"Let me ekshplain what we do. I ask, when was the last time of performing sex?"

He says this with a straight face. I assume the Doctor's question is medical and not a proposition. I try to think of the right answer. It's been many weeks since I slept with Monica. This could be hay-fever all over again, one wrong answer and I'll be on the street.

"A few days ago, I think." What a terrible answer.

"You think?" The Doctor says.

"Eight days back, 7.35am." These people like facts.

"OK, that's good." The Doctor makes a note.

I puzzle over why it's good. It seems terrible to me, disastrous. The truth is even worse. Nine weeks and two days I calculate, since Monica and I got it together. There have been a few kisses since then, some brushing against each other in corridors and plenty of looks that have lingered a second too long. It's driving me crazy. Occasionally, she sits with Williams and looks at me, like a test, seeing how I'll react. Other times she laughs at Williams' jokes like she's forgotten I'm there. Maybe she has.

The Doctor swivels in his executive-chair and describes the clinic's history and credentials in carefully moderated tones. I'm hungry. All I can think about is having an American-style turkey sandwich, and Monica, or perhaps both at the same time. His accent makes it difficult to follow the thread as it twists and tangles, embroidered with colourful medical terms. The tests are about blood, I get that much. I was never very good at Biology.

"Any side-effects please tell a nurse." The Doctor pauses.

"What type of side-effects?" I ask.

"Headaches, diarrhoea, nausea, vomiting or abnormal erections."

I think better about asking what classifies as an abnormal erection. The Doctor starts reading a document on his desk. There's a cough and I see the nurse holding the door open. She leads me down another hallway. The Doctor and nurse are brusque, but maybe that's the famed German efficiency, even though it feels cold to me.

"Your room," she says.

I half expect to hear the lock click as she leaves. Whatever happens this is going to be my home for the next five days, until I get my cash.

"Five days", I repeat aloud. I can do that. I'm good at waiting. I drum my fingers on the bed. After a few minutes, I tiptoe to the door, open it and peer down the corridor. A muted TV is playing further down the hall, throwing a kaleidoscope of colour over the floor. I walk towards it. The TV is bracketed to the wall above a small lounge with plastic-coated furniture. The dreadlocked man from earlier is talking to a blond guy.

"Hey man," dreadlock waves me over. "I'm Claude. This is Matthias."

Claude turns out to be a professional lab-rat backpacking across Europe. Matthias is Austrian. His English isn't great but it's much better than my German. I nod and smile as the two of them jabber away in German, pretending I understand some of it. Their words blur together, a language I should have learned months ago but never did. They revert to English for my benefit.

"Matthias has a trick," Claude winks.

"Warm water," Matthias says. Claude enthusiastically explains for him, dreadlocks swinging like metronomes as he talks.

"Two pints of lukewarm water before they come round. Afterwards —"

"—I have a talent for vomiting," Matthias says proudly.

"I'm hoping I get a placebo," I say.

Claude shakes his head. "This is a feed and bleed. No placebos. They're checking the drugs don't kill us."

"Don't they check the toilets? Wasn't that rule three?" I direct my comment at Matthias but Claude answers.

"They don't give a shit man," he explains. "The sooner they can prove the drugs don't kill people, the faster they can make some moolah." He rubs the tips of his fingers together.

We watch television. It's a thriller dubbed into German with English subtitles. It's weird watching famous actors speaking with somebody else's voice. Although sometimes I wonder who says the things that come out of my mouth. Like the time I said yes to Monica when I thought I was saying no. The adverts rise in volume, yelling at me in languages that make no sense, for products that have no appeal. Maybe I'm not a butterfly, but a fish out of water.

I'm still starving. Claude directs me to a vending machine. I haven't got much money and the only thing I can afford is a bag of yoghurt-coated peanuts. At least I don't have a nut allergy.

I go back to the bedroom and read a book about the future set in the past. I can't concentrate so I grab a pencil and start sketching. I draw Monica's hair. Long brown locks, perfectly in place. Of course, the grey pencil can't capture her hair's perfect shade of hazel, autumn leaves lit by the evening sun. Then I draw the curve of her face with a delicately turned-up nose and a hinted smile that she wears on her mouth and eyes. I dot a handful of freckles across the bridge of her nose, the seasoning that distinguishes her from airbrushed-models. The eyes are impossible though, given my feeble art skills. What can I say about them that doesn't sound like a cliché? Her eyes hold love, curiosity, passion, an entire world that I want to live inside. I screw up the sheet and try again. And again. I chuck the paper-balls at the bin and miss. Once upon a time, I was ok at art, better than maths and English, anyway. Thought it might be my thing, but I guess you have to practice. Ten thousand hours or whatever.

The food comes around on a trolley, at last! I eat while lying on the bed, starting with the ice cream because it is melting fast, and working backwards through the courses. Even though I'm starving, it is terrible quality. Gritty, tasteless, no flavour. Nice to see German hospitals are no better than the rest of the world in that regard. Twenty minutes later the nurse comes in with a colleague while I'm desperately chewing through the tough bread roll. She passes me a small paper container with two bright orange tablets that look like sweets, and a glass of water. Her colleague has a flashlight. I feel sick. Three more months in Berlin is worth five days as a white mouse. Putting one tablet on my tongue I swill it back with water and swallow hard. I prepare the second tablet and repeat. This time I nearly choke on the damn thing. The second nurse switches on the flashlight and holds my mouth open. She moves my head from side to side like an aggressive hairdresser.

Monica is a hair stylist. In fact, it all started with a cheap haircut in the flat. She massaged my head with some peppermint conditioner. Her fingers slid over me, applying pressure, caressing. Neither of us spoke and all I could hear was her breathing and my heart pounding. It was the most erotic thing ever. I couldn't stop thinking about her. The Beatles had a hairdresser as a girlfriend. I can't remember which one she went out with, may be more than one. That was Hamburg though.

The nurse lifts my tongue with a wooden spatula, its lolly-stick texture setting my teeth on edge. They say a few words in German and leave me, largely in the dark.

Restless, I wander back into the TV lounge. Claude is watching a programme in Italian. I wonder how many languages he can speak.

"Never go to Switzerland," he tells me. "Last thing I heard, they were stopping hearts. Fifteen seconds, thirty, then bam! Switch you back on. Scary."

"Why do you do it?" I ask.

"To see the world. I figure my body can take it for a couple of years. You?" His eyes are sharp. I like the fact that he has a plan, knows what he wants to do.

"Cash. I need to stay in Germany, but I can't get a job. Nothing that pays well enough anyway. A few gardening jobs, some construction stuff, that's it."

"A girl then?" Claude asks.

"No." I say that too firmly. "I mean, yes, there is, in the flat. Monica."

"Your girlfriend?" He asks.

"No, she's with Williams. My flatmate."

"Complicated."

We sit in silence for a few minutes and I check out the women on the sitcom. None of them could hold a candle to Monica. Claude starts cussing. I'm not sure what language. Wish I could do that, multi-lingual swearing.

"You got one of these yet?" he points at his gown that currently resembles a circus tent. I realise he's got a massive erection.

"Do you need me to do anything?" I say and then feel like a complete idiot. I go bright red.

"You could change to the soccer channel," he suggests.

I watch ten minutes of a dreary match. Claude is clearly uncomfortable. I leave him to whatever remedies are necessary and escape to my room.

With headphones on I listen to some music. I puzzle over why Monica stays with Williams. She says it's practical, but I'm not sure that's the right English translation. I think she means he's reliable, because he earns a steady paycheck, pays the bills on time. Maybe that's enough for her, or perhaps she's just waiting for me to step up. Unless Williams and I have got it all wrong, and she's the butterfly. Who knows which flower she might flit to next? I've thought about this a lot in the last week, sleeping rough on my way here, dreaming fitfully, when I managed to sleep. I never intended to hurt anyone. Something tells me Monica is a survivor; it's Williams and me that would be scarred. Whatever, I need to knuckle down and get some sort of career going and find my own place, then Monica will come with me. Maybe. Sometimes I feel like she's testing us, to see if we're good enough. It's easy enough for people who know what they want to do, simple to follow a passion if you have one. I just haven't found mine yet. As far as I know, Williams doesn't have a clue about Monica and me. Unless I missed that too, and it's why he recommended this place. I wonder if he knows what drugs they test here?

I have a favourite scene of Monica, and I start playing it in my mind, to distract myself. She's leaning on her elbows, looking at me in the bed. She has a halo from the late afternoon sun pushing its golden fingers through the curtain behind her. She smells of vanilla.

"You have a good heart," she whispers as she brushes my forehead, sweeping the hair out of my eyes. I keep that looping in my head. I take my time over each element, basking in the sensations, as I doze off.

***

I'm awake. My heart is pounding hard, much too fast, like I'm sprinting. I shout for the nurse. I don't want to get up and walk as my legs are shaking although I guess that's fear. The panic causes my heart to beat faster. I'm caught in a terrible spiral and imagine my heart exploding. My chest feels stretched taut like a drumskin, every beat reverberating into my arms and legs, thumping inside my head, like bass in a car stereo. I frantically try to calculate how fast a heart can go and whether it has a limiter like a car engine. I must be close to the redline. The nurse appears at the door stifling a yawn. I tell her the symptoms. She doesn't even make a note on the clipboard. I thought she was cold, but now she seems ruthless. How many patients have died under her care?

"Palpitations are not to worry."

I'm about to reply when she shushes me to take my pulse. Get it together, I tell myself, with a few extra words thrown in for good measure.

"If they remain in two hours you get aspirin."

"Two hours?" I manage to say, my tongue as dry as chamois leather.

"Relax." She manages an insincere smile as she shuts the door and I hear her slow footfalls down the hall.

I need to do something to avert my imminent death. Music is the only solution I can imagine; it seems to fix most things. Kept me sane during my parent's divorce. I pick the most calming album I can find and press play. I try breathing through my nose too, but I'm pretty crap at doing that, to be honest.

I remember the first time I saw Monica. I was waiting for Williams in a local pizzeria. He strolled in with Monica beside him, arms loosely hooked together and introduced her casually. She gave me a kind smile, and her hair swayed as she moved. Williams had been the slow kid at school, even I used to beat him in the tests and that's not saying much. He had opted for the role of school clown but wasn't that funny. Here in Germany he's built a new life with a good job and a great woman. It's not home, but it could be one day. Perhaps he needed one of the old crowd to validate his success. I came at his invitation because I had nothing else happening. Just lost my last job, but who wants to be a friggin' surveyor anyway? Sleeping on his couch, then sleeping with his girl. Not that I ever meant that to happen. Claude was right, it's complicated.

There's a track on the album I've never heard before, that starts with a wolf howling, a long mournful cry. Something in me responds, recognises the sound, understands the call. My chest vibrates. The heart tries to punch its way out and run blindly away. It thumps my legs to get them moving; it echoes in my wrists and threatens to burst out. Didn't werewolves think they were turning inside out when they transformed? That's what I feel like, stretched and taut. Maybe my old chrysalis is stretching and breaking, releasing something stronger and wilder. The howl resonates and now I'm cold, shivering. I try to think of heat, of summers gone. On the first hot day of the year my mother would take the Moroccan rug into the garden and hang it over the washing line. Then she would pulverise it. Can you beat a heart like a rug to scatter the dust? If you beat it hard enough, will it expel the impurities? Now my temperature is soaring. My mind is melting. I can't even concentrate when the grim reaper has his bony hands around my throat. I should have ticked the checkboxes properly. I should have known better. My heart tries to beat itself to death. I can't blame it. If I survive this, things will be different, they must be. I can't flip from one thing to the next, I need to have direction and purpose. The wolf needs to eat the butterfly.

Eventually the drums inside me slacken. I know what I must do. I get dressed and check out. The nurse shrugs as though she expected me to fail. She tagged me as a loser from the start.

"No money," she states.

"You're right," I say.

Outside, the moon is nearly full. I walk to the main road. The clinic is behind me and so is Berlin. Never liked the place anyway. Even the clouds box you in, not like Sydney's expansive blue skies. The wind is fierce, but I head right into it, instead of being shoved along at its whim. The wind fights back, pelting me with fistfuls of hard rain, but I push through. I don't have any money, but I do have what's left of a good heart, cleaned and purified. That's enough. I decide to walk to the nearest town and then head for the border. If a car comes, I'll ignore it. The time has come for me to take control of my destiny and stop flitting from one thing to another. Today has been one of those pivotal moments, a turning point, that's what they call it. I open-up a long-ranging stride to clear my head and hit a satisfying rhythm. I imagine myself lean, hard, and wild like a wolf. I walk down the central line on the tarmac. There are good reasons never to go back to Berlin, and the most important is that I won't wreck at least two lives. I can find work anywhere. It's tough to turn your back on the person you love, but sometimes that's what you must do.

I hear a car coming, move to one side and instinctively jerk my thumb out. Force of habit. For once the car pulls over. I jog to the window and after a few words in broken German I accept a ride into town. The car is warm and dry. It feels good to know I've decided though, and my new path is set. I can do anything when I apply myself. I'm a wolf now. My mind is set. I know Monica will be disappointed, but Williams won't care. Unless I have that the wrong way round. I stare at my reflection in the window. My face is lean, but a passing car's

lights pattern my skin in colour, and then they're gone.
"Where are you heading?" the driver asks.
"Berlin," I say.

Blue Monsters

I can remember when we were considered normal, twenty years ago. My mother used to take me to the Covered Market, and nobody stared. We would buy apples, a warm loaf and some cheese, then picnic in the meadow. I used to wear my summer dress that swirled when I spun like a ballerina. New friends came easily, and we would run, dance and sing in the honey-coloured light, then finally collapse, curling up in a nest of soft grass. My childhood memories were imprinted in that summer heat, when everything was malleable. As night approached, we would walk home and everything would cool and harden, fixing memories in place. I can still recall the joy of that life, before we became monsters.

Amy cries out and my memories fall away. She clutches the baby close to her chest while Martha tugs at her shawl. I shout from the ladder, propped against the apple tree.

"Leave her alone Martha," I say.

"What's it to you?" she snaps.

Carefully I step down the rungs, balancing the wicker basket. The apples rub against each other, jostling for space. I can see the orchard stretching over the crest of the hill that masks us from the normals. I don't know if they eat our apples or bake them into pies. My mother once told me that each apple has a blemish, but if you cut an apple crossways there's a star inside.

"There's still time," Amy says.

Martha leans against the base of the opposite ladder with that smirk, and shakes her head, knowingly. There are times when I believe we are dangerous, moments when I think the segregation makes sense. Mostly, these thoughts occur after dealing with Martha.

"There are rules," I say to Martha.

"Correct. It's my job to see they get followed," she answers.

Amy says nothing but rocks her baby, holding him close and shielding his head from Martha. The geneticists are clever people, I remind myself. They understand things I can't even pronounce. They must be right about us.

"They won't change," Martha declares. "They never do."

I put my arm around Amy's bony shoulder and suggest we get some barley water. We walk away and I hear Martha deride me as a slacker. The sun is dazzling, and we shield our eyes. Sunglasses are completely banned, even for the guards — too dangerous if we were to steal a pair. We make our way across the lawn. A second team are trimming yew hedges. At the porch we're permitted one drink each and a bottle of powdered milk for Amy's baby.

We sit in the corner. The woman at the counter is one of Martha's cohorts. She'll report back anything she hears. Amy's barley water sits untouched as her son feeds eagerly.

"Will they take him away?" she asks.

I sit forward and fold back the shawl so I can peer at his face. He has hazel eyes, with a hint of autumn gold around the edge. In every respect they're beautiful, but especially so because they're not blue.

"He can live a normal life Amy, he's blessed."

"He can do that here."

"A proper education and freedom to choose his clothes, his job, even his wife. None of that can happen here."

"I won't let him go." She has the petulant sound of a child.

That evening Martha glides into the Common Room like a queen. She has the palest blue eyes in our dormitory, almost white like rime frost. As Chief she gets extra coupons, warm water in the shower and cherry-red lipstick. In return she keeps the dormitory in order. I can never decide whether they deliberately pick the most aggressive to supervise or if the Chiefs are corrupted by their smidgen of power. There's no velvet glove with Martha.

    She pauses, a pace before me.

    "Double shift, earlies," she commands.

    Everyone turns to watch the confrontation.

    "I did as many baskets as anyone." I reply.

    "Did you hear that, girls? She's calling you lazy now."

    Martha's nostrils flare like a bull. I feel hollow, as though I'm made of china. We're secretly divided into a clique of cruel Martha followers and a silent majority. I've known for weeks that we would eventually clash. In my daydreams the majority step forward in my defence. Under the harsh light of the dormitory there's no movement. The colour seems to be draining out of the room leaving only Martha's diamond-hard eyes and red lips. I think that perhaps they're right. We're blue-eyed monsters. Genetically programmed to hate, to fight and kill.

    The scream shatters everything. There's a sound outside like a pig being slaughtered. Chaos follows. Martha is her usual step ahead. By the time I reach the corridor, Martha and her retinue are already returning from the garden. The white skin and gossamer dress make her look like a banshee, floating malevolently over the scrubbed boards. Her face is fixed in a wide smile.

    "See what you've done now," she says.

    I step outside. The glaring lights around the mansion produces an eerie twilight. Amy sits rocking and swaying. She lifts her blood-stained hands and holds them out to me, a howling son in her lap. Two black sockets disfigure his face. Amy chants a phrase like a prayer.

"I won't let him go, I won't let him go."

There's an empty bed in the dorm tonight where Amy used to sleep. The guards took her and the baby away. We won't see them again. When Amy's grief has dwindled, it'll be replaced by guilt. Living amongst us would be a vicious punishment, a daily reminder of her sins. I can't sleep. The world has turned against us. There's no hope of salvation, no release for good behaviour. The normals should kill us now and finish the job — except they can't, because that would make them monsters too. They must demonstrate compassion and hold us isolated, redundant and worthless. I've realised what they do with the apples we pick. They throw them away. Nobody would eat food tainted by our hands. There's probably a mountain of fruit in some corner of the country, kept under control by a handful of fat goats. I would poison the apples like an evil queen in a fairy-tale, but that would only kill the goats.

The orchard's trees stretch out in parallel lines, aiming at a horizon that seems further than infinity. I'm inside an old tree reaching for the highest fruit, balancing precariously on thin branches. My mind is busy on a scheme to start a secret distillery to make some alcohol and blow our minds every night. Oblivion would be welcomed to the dormitory like a long-lost friend.

"Geordie likes you," whispers the girl holding my ladder.

We don't know the guards by name. Each one is marked out by a distinguishing feature like a scar, a tattoo or an accent.

"The way he watches." She glances over her shoulder.

"Maybe he'll whisk me off to Paris for the weekend?" I smile.

"He knows where they took Amy," the girl says.

I look down. It's not far but the branches are worse than claws. I stretch for the furthest apple and deliberately let my foot slip. I pull in my hands to cover my face but only one side is protected as a branch wrenches my other arm behind me. The plunge happens fast and hurts. I don't register the shouts and calls. When I try to move, my side hurts, far more than I intended. Martha holds back as Geordie supervises the scene.

"Get the stretcher," he says to Martha. She doesn't move until he gives her a mouthful of slang and abuse. I love the sound of it but I can't understand a word. I start to laugh but breathing is agony.

He kneels beside me and turns my arm over gently and squeezes my hand. It's the first act of kindness I've experienced in two years. I can feel my eyes welling with tears.

"They'll be here soon." Geordie says.

"Amy?" I ask.

Geordie looks me in the eye. They don't do that. Some of the girls say eye contact is forbidden; I've always thought it was fear. They've been told so long that we're monsters, why shouldn't they believe it? I stare back. His eyes dilate and I know he understands.

"You'll be in the same wing," he confirms.

Martha comes with two attendants carrying a khaki stretcher. They lay it beside me and Geordie stands up. He barks commands at Martha's team. The pain becomes intense as they shift me on to the canvas. The sun blazes so I shield my egg-shell eyes with one hand.

When I wake, it's night. Someone is hissing.

"Is that you?" Amy's voice.

I see a silhouette on the bed next to me. I can't make out her face.

"It's me, Amy," she says and giggles.

My sight is clearing. Her arms are hooked up to tubes. She must be high, dosed on painkiller. Croakily I say her name and reach out my arm. We hold hands like lovers without saying another word. I shift gently to see what hurts. I'm not connected to a tube, but my torso has layers of soft bandage wrapped around it. The skin on the left side of my face feels rough and sore. A male nurse passes through the hall. Amy quickly pulls her hand away and we both pretend to be asleep. After he's gone, she brushes my arm and pushes something into my hand.

"Hide this," she says.

"What is it?"

"A life," she answers. "A real life."

In the morning she's gone. I inspect her gift in the latrine. It's a small plastic container with two compartments. I slowly unscrew one side and find a contact lens, brown as chocolate. Outside of here, this gift would be precious. Inside it's a valuable curiosity offering the dream of escape while ignoring the issues. There's still the challenge of getting from here to the normals' world. Brown eyes or not the guards know me, plus we only have our uniforms to wear. I will have to use it wisely.

***

It's dark, and Geordie's recovering his breath. My ribs still ache, but two months since the accident they're finally beginning to heal. I thought I would feel different tonight, I wasn't expecting to enjoy this, but I have. The pleasure fills me with guilt. I think about Amy. I caress Geordie's neck and whisper something I think he wants to hear. I need to keep him wrapped here a little longer. Martha needs more time to complete her escape.

She was suspicious at first.

"You can do more than me out there." I said.

She raised an eyebrow.

"You're harder than I am. You know how to get people on your side. You can change things. You won't get caught."

"Well, you're right about that," she said.

"Make something good happen Martha." I passed her the lenses.

I wasn't sure what she was going to do next. Martha put her arms around me and gave me a hug. It was genuine, warm. Then she turned back to frost.

"Thursday night, Geordie's on shift."

"I'll see to it." I said.

Of course, it makes things a little easier here too. I'd be a liar if I didn't admit I'd thought about that. With Martha gone we might work together and show them that we're human after all. She leant me some of her things. I look at her bright red lipstick, smeared across Geordie.

I'm hot, sticky as honey. I want to curl up like a fossil in this grass and watch clouds sail around the moon, but this is not the time. Geordie is going to sit up. I roll over him and caress his hair. My other hand brushes his chest.

"We're not finished yet," I tell him.

Shadow Day

Señor Herrera had made the school's toughest football-player cry, sentencing him to a shadow day at *Buffappa*, where the floors were awash with cow blood and the stench could be smelt ten blocks away. When it was his turn, Señor smiled wickedly at Raoul, *A special one for you* he said, and Raoul shrugged. Señor pushed a sheet across his desk with the name Miller, and a telephone number.

Raoul called, and it was arranged that Miller would collect him on the way to the job. Miller told him to bring an overnight bag, with jeans, tee-shirt, and a fleece. Miller was vague about the work.

When the truck rolled up, Raoul saw a blonde in the jump seat, mid-twenties, athletic and tanned, beaming a smile at him. A man that he assumed was Miller sat behind the wheel, but was much older than the woman, and it was clear they weren't together. Raoul made the sign of the cross and thanked the Lord for blessing him with good looks and fortune.

Miller talked incessantly about his family during the journey, making it hard for Raoul to connect with the blonde, who was called Jessica. They checked into a motel in the middle of nowhere and ate some tepid burrito's next to a thread-bare pool table.

"You like to play?" Raoul stuck his thumb over his shoulder towards the line of cues, directing the question at Jessica.

"Nah," she said. "Not my thing."

"I'll give you a game," Miller stood and went to rack the balls. "You can break," he said.

The cues tips were shot to hell, but Raoul took the best

he could find and twirled it like a baton. He asked Jessica another question, forcing her to look his way as he delivered a hammer-blow for the break.

"What's the job? What are we doing tomorrow?"

Miller was staring at the balls as they crashed and collided off each other, studying the angles, leaving Jessica to answer.

"We've got to sand down some fibre-glass and wood, patch up some industrial damage. It's a routine task. You like to surf, Raoul?"

"Sure," he slammed the number five ball into the corner pocket.

"Any good?" Miller asked

"I can make two or three cuts, throw in a hard cutback on a better day," he said.

Jessica waited for him to miss before she continued, "Then you've fixed a surf-board before, right?"

He nodded.

"Same thing tomorrow. Sand, fill and polish," she smiled.

"Are you a surfer Jessica? I can see you on a beach." Raoul smiled, pleased at his mental image.

"Nah, ocean isn't my thing. Too many jocks," she said, although Raoul wasn't entirely sure that she hadn't said jerks.

"She's in a band," Miller said. "Guitar and vocals." He messed up his shot, leaving Raoul with a clear break.

"Awesome," Raoul said, rapidly potting the balls.

"What about you Raoul. Is there a girl waiting somewhere?" Jessica asked.

He didn't answer immediately, sliding the pool stick between his fingers, rehearsing a shot. He punched the ball low with a fistful of back spin, and the cue ball shot back across the table, while his target cannoned off the corner cushion, missing its destination.

"I'm free. No ties."

Miller swigged his beer, and said, "Really? Good-looking guy like you? Can't be short of options."

Raoul made a face at Miller, "May be when I find the right girl, you know?"

Miller nodded and watched as Raoul methodically cleared the table, never missing a chance to use a power shot where he had a choice. He looked up triumphantly to find Jessica shifting from her chair.

"Guys, I'm gonna hit the sack early. Eight a-m for breakfast?"

"Winner buys tequila..." Raoul hastily stepped across her path to constrain Jessica's exit.

"Nah, thanks. May be tomorrow." She lifted the cue like a parking barrier, escaping the room's corner. Raoul watched her stride across the lobby. He shrugged.

***

The road ran straight across the Badlands, and they slowly reeled in the distant mountains. There was a wind farm to one side, and Raoul watched the giant propellers in their slow-motion rotations and imagined the world upside down, the turbines propelling the land gently across the fixed sky.

Miller switched on the left blinker, even though there was no sign of a turn.

"We here?" Raoul asked.

"Close," Miller said, exiting the road onto a narrow track.

Through the windshield were the turbines, looking taller and thicker by the minute, a white forest of giant metal trees. They came to a locked gate, with a tiny hut beside. It looked unmanned, but a yawning guard stepped out, acknowledged Miller, then removed a padlock and pushed the entrance wide. Jessica glanced down at a map and pointed.

"That one," she said.

Miller pulled alongside a towering mast that vanished like a beanstalk into the clouds. Jessica and Miller jumped out of the truck without a word.

"What ya waiting for?" Jessica called.

Heat and dust swirled around her as Raoul walked to the truck's rear where Jessica was unzipping a large canvas bag. She lifted a tangled cobweb of tools on a belt, and stepped into it, clipping the plastic locks together around her waist. Raoul saw a circle of yellow and orange rope coiled like a snake. Miller emerged wearing a belt that matched Jessica's. He handed Raoul another.

"Get this on, and we'll adjust," Miller said. "You'll need this too," he tossed him a hard-shelled helmet, with a pair of gloves inside.

Raoul felt sucker-punched.

"It's just routine maintenance," Miller said.

"On that," Jessica pointed up and Raoul lifted his head to watch the huge blade sweeping a hundred feet above their heads. He had to shade his eyes because of the sun, and the wind hurled stinging dust at his face.

"It's a huge surfboard.," Jessica added. "Fibreglass exterior on a wood substructure, in need of care and attention."

Miller pulled the straps tight on Raoul's belt and checked his helmet, before passing him a bucket filled with tools.

"You're not scared, are you?" Jessica smiled sweetly at him.

He shook his head.

"You should be," Miller said. "It's fear that keeps you safe."

Miller opened an oval door at the base of the mast, and Raoul was surprised to see the turbine was hollow inside. They began climbing a ladder that might seem flimsy if you were replacing a light fitting in your ceiling. Miller led, then Raoul, with Jessica at the tail.

"How many rungs?" Raoul managed to say.

"Three hundred to three fifty. More in a Vestas V112. Shouldn't take us more than six or seven minutes to get to the top," Jessica said.

"There's three sections," Miller added. "We're in the base now, then we'll go through a trapdoor into the middle. You might notice the tower swaying more in the next section. Don't let it bother you."

Raoul tried to focus on holding a solid grip on each rung. His arms were tiring as he clenched each bar too tightly. He was fit though, and in the final section, he began to find a rhythm.

"Stay put until I call you, Raoul," Miller said, lifting the final trapdoor, and clambering on to the roof.

"What about the blades?" Raoul asked Jessica, his voice echoing ominously as it fell towards ground level.

"Locked and feathered. They'll flex but won't rotate."

Raoul could see blue sky in the open portal above him and listened to the roaring wind. His legs were shaking, and he hoped Jessica would not see. After a command from Miller, he climbed the last rungs, pushing his head out of the mast.

"Climb on to your knees, and stay down until I've clipped you," Miller said.

Raoul pushed himself on to the slippery surface, where he crouched and panted like a scared dog. The sunlight reflecting off the white surface was blinding, and he hung his head low. The roof reminded him of the top of his mother's Kitchen-Aid mixer that sat unused but shining in their kitchen. He noticed a white rail around the edge of the mast top, only a couple of inches high, that wouldn't even stop a prairie dog falling off. There was a tug at his waist, and then another.

"Krabs on and locked. They're your safety lines. You can stand up and admire the view," Miller told him. Raoul lifted his head, and slowly moved his hands off the surface, and sat back on his haunches. Jessica was already standing, spooling through a reel of rope. Miller was staring at him.

"You OK?"

"Sure," Raoul said, his voice croaky.

Miller grabbed Raoul's hands and partially supported his weight while dragging him to his feet. He kept hold for a few seconds, until it seemed like Raoul wouldn't topple.

"It's windy," Raoul said.

"That's why they put them here," Jessica said. "This is mild, twelve to fourteen knots at most. They're rated at a touch over 30 miles-per-hour. Not that you'd find us here then."

"Spectacular view, eh?" Miller said.

"Better get to work," Jessica walked over to Raoul, and began hooking and knotting a rope to his belt. She gave rapid instructions about do's and don'ts, but Raoul registered nothing.

"Safety Briefing over. Right, it's easier to go backwards," Jessica told him.

They were standing side by side at the edge of the platform.

"All you do is lean back," she said, demonstrating, and suddenly she was gone, slipping off the platform as easily as flopping into a feather bed.

Miller faced him. "Your turn. Lean, further, further…"

Raoul fell like a bad dream, a shock of acceleration and fear. He swallowed bile as he decelerated to a bouncing stop next to Jessica. She was sitting in her straps as comfortably as though she were in a swing at the park.

Jessica talked him through the lateral movement they needed to reach the turbine, using their toes to push gently off the mast's outer shell. The blade was huge, and twisted, curled like a wave.

"We're looking for a dark spot, or a hole," she said, caressing the sleek white skin, and steadying herself, as a pummel of wind caused them to sway and rock. Raoul closed his eyes for a moment, told himself this would soon be over.

"Got it, see?" Jessica said, forcing Raoul to open his eyes. There was a discoloured spot on the blade.

"What is it?" he asked.

"Lightning. They have protection systems, but still get hit. Nothing else this height around here," she gestured with her arm, swaying slightly. She pulled a small compact camera from a pocket and snapped a picture.

"That's the before. If moisture gets in, the balsa rots and then the whole thing comes down. Hand me the sander, will you?" Raoul looked in the bucket. He realised he was holding his rope with both hands, and nervously let go with one hand to pass the tool to Jessica. Accidentally, he brought a spare sanding disc out of the bucket, caught on his glove, and it fell. He watched it plummet, spinning and lifting as the wind toyed with it like a killer whale with a seal.

"Miller says it doesn't matter if you fall fifteen feet or five hundred. Result's the same. You get longer to think about it, that's all."

Jessica was hard at work sanding, head down. She reminded Raoul of someone. The way she screwed her face tight when she was concentrating, and the cute kink in her nose.

Looking up, Jessica scanned the horizon. "Cumulonimbus," she said, pointing. Raoul turned to see a rising column of dark cloud.

"How long before it gets here?"

Jessica, waved a hand dismissively, "At least an hour."

Raoul was blown by a gust to one side and began swinging like a pendulum, gathering more distance each time. He shifted his weight in the straps, but that generated more momentum. Jessica was filling the hole and keeping very still. Raoul made the mistake of looking down, then pulled his head back sharply and his vision went grey for a moment. The swaying stopped abruptly, and Jessica was holding his forearm.

"Try not to gain speed," she said.

Raoul was almost in tears.

"Señor Herrera used to be my Spanish tutor," Jessica said, releasing his arm.

"Is that...?" Raoul tried to assemble the sequence of events leading to his suspension three hundred feet in the air next to a crazy blonde. Jessica said nothing.

"Did I see you once, in his office?" Raoul said. "I'm sure we've met."

Jessica shook her head. "We've not met. The lessons were at my home."

The blade creaked, straining like a sail. Miller crackled over a walkie-talkie, warning Jessica about the storm.

"We're good." She rolled the volume down.

She caught Raoul staring at her. "Do I remind you of someone?"

He thought hard.

"That's a long mental list you seem to be running through, Raoul."

"Yes," he said. "Hazel, my ex-girlfriend. Bonita. She was lovely."

***

Jessica was finishing. The storm was still a long way off, but the wind speed was increasing, and it was getting bumpy. The turbine was desperate to start spinning, with those long, guillotine-blades.

Raoul swore, as the wind pushed him clumsily into the side of the mast, bashing his thigh.

"Time to make our exit," Jessica said. "I'm going to climb up and then help you in when I'm secure. Hang tight."

Raoul nodded and gripped the rope with both hands, watching Jessica shimmy back towards the platform. Part way up she paused and turned to shout a question over the wind.

"If Hazel was so lovely, why did you leave her?"

"I wasn't ready to get tied down, you know?"

Jessica nodded and returned to her climb. At the top, Raoul watched Miller help pull her on to the platform. She clipped her safety lines on to the rail, and stood talking to Miller, who disappeared. It looked like he might have headed back to the hatch, but it was hard to see from this angle. Jessica waved her walkie-talkie in the air and gestured to his belt. There was a static buzz, and he found his own device strapped in a velcro pocket. It wasn't easy to wriggle out, and it meant releasing a hand from the rope again, but he managed it.

"Can you hear me?" Jessica was saying.

Raoul pressed the big green button and said "Yes."

"Great." Jessica answered. "Watch carefully, and don't move yet." She said.

He didn't like the sound of that. He covered his face with one hand to shield his eyes from the light and study her movements. He saw her unclipping two metal devices, and dropping them over the side, they sailed past him, and bounced in the air, jangling against each other and the side of the mast. They were connected to him by thin yellow ribbon and hung suspended thirty feet below.

"Those were your security lines," Jessica said. "If the knot here fails, or the rope frays, you'll fall to your death."

He pressed the green button, but Jessica overrode his communication. "I've been told I look like my sister. Although Hazel doesn't look so good these days. It's tough being a single mum, when you're barely eighteen. You left her dangling..."

Raoul began to frantically haul himself up the rope, hand over hand. Jessica leant over the edge, and started to apply pressure, first one way and then the other, until the rope began its pendulum motion again, swinging him in and out of the shadows made by the blades and the sun. Raoul crashed into one of the blades and fell the few feet he had gained.

"You don't want to get tied down, you say? Your wish is granted, Raoul. By the way, the knot looks surprisingly loose. When you climb, I'd advise you to do it very slowly, or the rope might come slithering down."

"I'm sorry," Raoul shouted.

Jessica moved away from the edge.

Raoul felt the wind rousing itself, like a toddler, ready to throw a tantrum. The rope creaked, and below him the safety lines jangled.

The walkie-talkie crackled one more time.

"Forgot to say, the turbine restarts in five minutes."

Jessica sat on the platform next to Miller. They looked at the knot, which was still tight as a fist.

"What if he has a heart attack?" Miller said.

"He won't. He's built like a bull."

"He's going to hate you," Miller added, nonchalantly.

Jessica shrugged. "Shadow days are meant to be educational. He's going to learn how to cope on your own, when you're scared and inexperienced. It's a great lesson, he might thank us."

"Yeh, right." Miller said.

At the end of the rope, Raoul sobbed. He clung to the precarious lifeline and reflected on his many poor decisions.

"I'll change!" he cried into the sky.

When the tears were finally swept away by the ravenous wind, and his breathing became less ragged, Raoul began the gruelling journey to redemption. Inches at a time, he squeezed up the thin rope, blistered hands leaving blood stains inside his gloves. At the top, too weak to make the final push, he dangled in the void until Miller and Jessica pulled him on to the platform. He lay flat on his back, drenched with sweat.

"The turbine didn't start," he said, finally, gulping air.

"I lied about that. People don't always tell the truth, do they?" Jessica said. "That's two things you've learnt today."

"You should have been a teacher," Miller said.

Raoul made the sign of the cross and blessed the Lord for granting him a second chance. He wondered if it was too late to repair the damage with Hazel. He wanted to ask, but his words were gone, as though the wind had stolen them to scatter across the desert like seeds.

One Page Ahead

"I love your fingers."

"I like them too," she said, with her strong accent.

He found it hard to tell if she was being ironic. The tangled hair that shadowed her eyes made them hard to read. She was a closed book.

"They're so slender," he held her hand. "Like an artist. Can you play the piano?"

"I had lessons, molti anni fa."

Her fingers demonstrated some patterns using his chest as the keyboard and then, tantalisingly, his thigh. She stopped abruptly and tilted her head back to fix him with her gaze. "I never learned the right tune for regret."

Adrian was unsure if she was teasing, or if she knew more than he had told her.

"You are really pale," she said. That was an understatement. Adrian was white as marble beside her terracotta skin. Yet this had been one of the hottest summers on record.

"I don't get out much." Grief was not a subject to talk about this early in a relationship. "Tell me something," he said.

"What?"

"Anything in Italian."

"Allora, e strano ma ho sognato che siamo andati all'Inferno…"

Her intonation rose and fell as a melody. The words meant nothing to him, but he loved the tune and the instrument. His hand stroked through her hair. The guilt that had crushed him for months was almost forgotten. Finally, his luck seemed to have changed. It was a delirious feeling.

"Are you an-gry?" she asked, reverting to English.

"No."

"We eat?"

"Hungry. Hun-gry," he stressed the opening syllable. "Not angry."

Slipping a tee-shirt over his head he yawned his way down the narrow hallway to the kitchen. He poured two glasses of orange juice that were only just past the sell-by-date. Then he sliced in half a pink grapefruit that had survived longer than anything else.

"I'm allowed to be happy," he said to a picture clipped to the fridge.

With breakfast loaded on a tray Adrian returned to nudge open the bedroom door. The bed covers were strewn wide, and he was alone again. For a few seconds he stood in disbelief. Adrian tried to think logically through the possibilities. It was feasible she'd slipped out while he was in the kitchen. He studied the pillows for a black hair as evidence of her existence. Nothing. A moment ago, he'd been the lead in a romance novel, and now he was trapped in a ghost story.

Perhaps he was going insane. For several weeks he'd been torn by doubts about the nature of his life. Strange co-incidences had been shaping his world, although he'd not been able to thread the narrative together. Adrian felt like a character in a story, each step dragging him closer to a fate someone else had written. He imagined readers watching him stumble, their laughter echoing faintly, almost imperceptibly, bouncing off the walls of his flat. He walked to the shower, observing that the front door was still locked from the inside.

***

Monday was hotter than hell. The air conditioning in his office block was due to be installed next month. He simmered at his desk, forcing thoughts about sensible practicalities and organising his tasks into chunks of measured reasoning. He was aware that his colleagues still avoided him as though sudden death were contagious. It was six months since the accident. Everyone blamed him for the death of his brother, including himself.

The conversation stopped when he entered the kitchen. It was the usual cluster of folk, plus the top salesman. They'd not met since the accident.

"We're really sorry Adrian," the salesman said. "It was a terrible accident. Nobody could have done anything."

"Uh-huh." He could survive these conversations as long as he kept his answers short. The wound was still raw. Even worse, the salesman was wrong. Somebody could have done something.

"An Alfa-Romeo, wasn't it?" the salesman asked. "Your car? An Alfa."

"Yes."

The salesman shook his head, knowingly. "Italian," he said, as though that explained everything. Adrian left, before the scene turned ugly. He knew there was only one person who could have prevented the accident, and that person's name began with the letter A.

At six o'clock Adrian spilled on to the evening streets. The dark-eyed Italian girl lingered in his thoughts as waves of commuters pushed him towards the underground. Somewhere between Clay Road and the Parade he had a notion that he was being watched. He tried to dismiss the sensation, yet the feeling grew as he approached the gaping entrance of the station. The escalator swallowed him, and he spiralled into the depths. He turned to look at the blank faces ranged behind. Most people glanced away at his hard stare.

Everyone looked the same, he decided, a meaningless crowd with no colour or detail.

The temperature soared beneath the city. Adrian felt a bead of sweat tracing the hollow of his spine like a phantom finger. The air was dense and he walked to the end of the platform and angled his body away from the shadows of the tunnel, to study the other passengers. At first, they were just a faceless blur, and he tried to find new stories in the crowd; the man with a plaster on his face, the skinny teenager with Ugg boots and a frayed coat. Nobody stepped out of their role as a stereotype, leaving Adrian the focus of the scene and still experiencing that sickening feeling of observation, as though he were a white mouse under scrutiny by a scientist.

Forcing himself to relax, he closed his eyes and breathed deeply. There was an evocative smell. Adrian recognised the scent but struggled to name it. Bread, petrol, and his ex-girlfriend's Mitsouko perfume were the only smells he could consistently identify. It felt like if only he could recognise the scent, it might be the clue that made everything fall into place. A distant rattle and the onset of wind finally heralded the approach of the train.

He found a place to lean inside the dirty, claustrophobic carriage. His breathing became ragged, and a few people began to look in his direction. The closest edged away, as though he were cursed or haunted. He burst off the train at his stop and sprinted up the stairs, gulping down clean air as he emerged under the night sky. The roads were bright with streetlights. The scent had gone but the sensation of being observed was harder to shake. Slowly he walked to his flat and paused before the red front door.

He stared at the unfamiliar scratches on his metal-plate keyhole. Once inside, he followed a trail of biscuit crumbs down the hall, noting their size and composition. The kitchen was a mess. Had he really left it like this in the morning? He inspected the rotting window frame, pushing a finger deep into the wood to watch it splinter. The close focus on each element built the feeling of suspense to an alarming level. His heart was racing. All he could see were the sparse details, creating a sense of foreboding that hid the bigger picture. He considered that since the first appearance of the black-eyed girl a few days before, his story had moved from romance to crime and seemed to be creeping towards horror. He carefully examined every inch of the flat, yet the only thing inside was the stifling heat.

***

That night, he slept beneath a cotton sheet that provided a thin illusion of protection. Soon he was dreaming. He walked up a hill with the dark-eyed girl waiting at the summit. There was somebody behind him. He could feel the pursuer gaining with every step. Glancing over his shoulder he saw a distinctive grey trench coat, a size too large, wrapped around a tall frame. The figure leaned forward and strode effortlessly up the hill. He knew that if he broke into a run their unwritten rule would be broken, and his pursuer would devour the distance between them. He strained to walk faster. Although the figure's face was indistinct beneath messy brown hair, he knew who it was. He didn't want to answer his questions. Approaching the girl, he looked into her eyes, and she smiled, sadly.

"It is a strange thing," she sang in her flute-voice, "to be haunted by your brother."

"What are you doing here?" he asked her.

She ran a gentle hand through his hair but said nothing.

"You never told me your name," Adrian said.

"Why don't you take a guess?" she suggested.

"Regret? Guilt? Death?"

The flat shook him awake. Every five and a half minutes, night or day, heavy traffic thundered past and rattled anything capable of being broken. Normally he could sleep through it, but tonight it felt as though his life was crumbling as surely as the foundations. He turned over in the bed, knotting himself in the sheet and drifting back to sleep. A single horn-blast woke him again, the accident on playback in his mind, his brother rigid in the passenger seat before the impact.

He stood naked in the bedroom, waiting for the fear to dissipate. Returning to the kitchen he found a bottle of holiday-Calvados and sloppily poured himself a drink. He'd read enough books to know that one badly poured glass would result in him crashing to the floor blind drunk in the next paragraph. On his right was a clip-frame holding a snapshot. He studied his brother's face.

"Who's the girl?" he asked the photo. "Did you send her?"

After waiting a few seconds for a reply, he hurled his glass into the wall then pointed at the smashed fragments.

"You didn't expect that, did you?" he said.

***

On Wednesday, during a meeting, he found himself doodling spirals of ink-black hair and he floundered when the client asked him a direct question. Afterwards, the manager called him to his office.

"How are you coping Adrian?" he began.

"Fine."

"You seem a little…" the manager paused, searching for the appropriate word, "…distant. You look like you haven't slept in weeks. We're concerned about you." He corrected himself, "I'm concerned about you. I need to know if everything is OK."

"Am I supposed to answer honestly?" Adrian said.

The manager nodded, but Adrian couldn't afford to lose his job.

"Then I'm fine," he lied. "Getting better all the time."

"People are beginning to comment about your work. And the way you look. We're worried." He paused to give Adrian the option to react, which he didn't take. "I like to think we've been more than supportive, and I've kept you away from any time-critical projects. Is there anything more you think we should be doing?"

"No, you've done all I expected." Adrian said.

"Are you seeing anyone?" the manager asked.

"What do you mean?" Adrian thought of the dark-eyed girl.

"A counsellor or perhaps a psychiatrist?"

"Doctor, doctor," Adrian said. "I think I'm a pair of curtains."

"Pull yourself together man. Bo-Bom." The manager smiled, glad that he knew the punchline. "It might help. I know someone who's good."

"What's the name?" Adrian asked.

"They call him Il Dottore. I've got his details here somewhere."

Adrian had no intention of calling the man but was struck by another strange fact. Only he had a name. The people in Adrian's life had become caricatures: his brother, the salesman, the manager and doctor. Even the dark-eyed girl didn't have a name. Like a story. Whatever was going to happen would be about him alone. Nobody could save him, not the manager, his brother and certainly not the readers. They wanted a dramatic ending, their pound of flesh. They weren't here for redemption, they craved ruin and disaster, to earn their moral superiority. He'd read enough stories and felt the same way, enjoying the game of second guessing the narrator. Only the dark-eyed girl might help him, but that path was shadowed and filled with as much threat as promise.

He left work early and took the bus home, reluctant to use the tube again. Inside his flat there was a hint of the nameless odour. It was indistinct and after a minute he could no longer smell anything, no matter how hard he tried. He felt violated, as though somebody was inside his home and his head, eavesdropping on his most private thoughts. He couldn't bear to stay in the flat any longer. On impulse, he headed for the Unicorn. It was crowded, and he had to wriggle to the bar like a maggot through rotting meat. He waited with money in hand. The attractive female staff chose customers at random. People either side of him got served while he waited. It seemed impossible to catch their eye, and he waved his money in the air. They seemed to be the only people who weren't treating him as the protagonist in the tale.

A man turned to him.

"I've seen you before," the man said. "I knew your brother."

Adrian was about to make a denial when the man added,

"He was one of the good guys. I'm sorry."

"Big brothers. They're meant to look after us, aren't they?" Adrian asked.

"I guess?"

"Who looks after them?" Adrian said this too loud,

causing a gap to open around the two of them. He began to shake.

"Don't blame yourself, mate. It was an accident," the man said quietly.

"How do you know? You weren't there." Adrian was shouting now.

The man reached out to Adrian, but he'd already gone, thrusting his unwanted money back into a pocket.

***

In Finborough Avenue the air was heavy, preparing for a long-needed storm. Adrian took that as a sign that he was approaching the final climatic scene. A bus groaned past with a large advert of a winking man on the side. It was the face of his brother. Adrian snatched an empty coke-can off the pavement and hurled it after the bus. There was nobody around. Adrian spread his arms wide and shouted to an invisible audience.

"You think you know what's happening, don't you?"

The bus pulled to a stop a few hundred yards down the avenue.

"You're one page ahead, that's all," he yelled.

Then he ran towards the tube station.

The red and white neon sign buzzed as Adrian burst into the lobby. He jumped over the barrier. There was a flicker in the depths of the station that could have been a black skirt, if that was what you wanted to see. Leaping a handful of steps at a time, he hurtled down the escalator.

A whirr announced the approach of the next train. Landing heavily, Adrian staggered and used his momentum to carry him forward. From the rush of air, he could feel the train approaching from the north. It would be another commuter train, crammed with hot people to vent from the train like steam. He swerved left, not ready to face so large a visible audience, and found himself on a near deserted platform. There was one woman lurking in the shadows, her face turned away. Calming himself, he moved towards her, unsure if it was the woman he sought. After all this effort, he had no idea what to say.

"Perhaps I'll let you decide," he murmured.

The sound of his feet echoed, and the lingering fragrance was back. Finally, he recognised the smell. It was oil. Clean and clear, sweet as honey, the smell of new oil. Not the dirty stuff the colour of midnight that poured over the road after the accident. Not the creeping oil that mixed with petrol and billowed black smoke when it caught alight, incinerating the knot of his shattered Alfa-Romeo. Thrown clear, Adrian had lain on the road with a twisted limb and seen it all. The wreck, the fire, and his brother trapped inside, looking at him. Like a scene from a story.

The woman began to stir. He was twenty paces away and could see the coils of hair. There was no mistake; this was his vanishing dark-eyed girl. Adrian wondered if it had been a mistake to follow her down here, if that had been his choice, or if someone else was pushing the narrative. Was it his brother, or the unseen readers who were after him? If he left now, could he seize his choice, decide his own fate? There were so few words left to be said, and Adrian knew no character can outrun the predetermined ending. For a moment Adrian hesitated, and the girl turned, her eyes pulling him in, with those slender fingers outstretched. He embraced his dark-eyed guide. Their hands locked tight, her grip like iron, and her other arm encircled him as with one motion she swept him aloft. Her lips brushed his ear, and she whispered.

"I am..." but Adrian did not wait to hear the final word

and seized a kiss, intoxicated by her scent, and ready to finish this tale. They whirled around but it seemed as though they were at the centre of everything, and it was the station that span around their fixed point. Adrian felt as though he were falling. The girl's eyes were no longer dark. They were brilliant white, dazzling, engulfing. They seemed to get bigger and bigger until he could see nothing else. His blood roared as it hurtled through his veins, loud as an approaching train. Then he heard his brother calling his name, a high-pitched cry that began like the sound of squealing brakes, and fell into a deeper pitch, more like the call of a lighthouse summoning a lost ship.

"I'm on my way," he whispered.

Other People's Wives

They'd walked in silence since they left the truck. It was hot and sweat had soaked the back of each man's shirt. Naveed shifted the gun to give his aching arm some relief, then stopped. He turned to face down the valley, as though searching for something, rather than an excuse for a break. He nodded at the truck, lit-up like a star by the dazzling sunlight.

"Why did you stick with Chevy?" he said.

"Ain't goin' aluminum. Ford are crazy if they think the F150 is gonna sell without steel," Jeff spat to punctuate his comment.

"Military-Grade al-you-min-ium alloy," Naveed said, carefully pronouncing each syllable in his English accent. "It's light weight, you get more power, more miles to the gallon. It's the future."

"I ain't stoppin' yer from buyin' one. Might suit a pretty foreign boy like you," Jeff replied, with his distinctive, rasping voice. "Let's see what happens when you hit the first critter bigger than a jackrabbit." Jeff sucked in a gut full of air and inflated his barrel-chest until he looked twice the width of Naveed.

The third man gave a cough, and his two colleagues turned, waiting for the plaid-clad Giant to pronounce a verdict. His faded baseball cap shielded his eyes and made any expression hard to read.

"When you two have finished admiring the view..." he said, then turned back to the trail zigzagging across the hillside. His black gun tote was slung casually over a shoulder. Naveed followed immediately after Giant, shotgun resting uneasily over his arm, with the barrels pointing down as he'd been shown. Around his waist he wore a canvas belt with pockets crammed full of red cartridges, and he still wasn't convinced they wouldn't explode if they got too hot. Behind him, Jeff lifted his sunglasses and wiped his face. His gun rested comfortably over a thick forearm, but he let out a curse as he set off. Naveed glanced back.

"Damned knee. Wasn't built for this," Jeff said.

"Should have bought one made of steel," Naveed said dryly.

"Too many motorbikes, too much football," Jeff replied.

"Too old," came a third voice, drifting down trail from Giant.

A bright green lizard watched intently as the party brushed past his boulder.

Naveed asked, "Are any lizards poisonous?"

"Only to eat," Jeff snorted and flicked the barrel of his gun in the lizard's direction and it darted away.

Naveed kept his eyes down, nervous of any rustle, stepping over sticks on the path. Jeff kept up a rumble of curses as he limped up the trail in his leather boots.

"You better be right about this Nav," he said. "Be a shame to come all this way and have nothing to shoot."

Naveed ignored the sly change in tone on the word nothing. "This is the place. I googled it, and cross-ref'd the GPS data exhausts."

"He knows his tech stuff," Giant said. "You should see the beta-glucan charts on my grain."

"Mister Precision Agriculture," Jeff said in a mock English accent, "How did we farm without you?"

Naveed resisted the bait.

They approached a small summit, hoping it was the peak and

not the reveal for another ascending section of path. Giant arrived first.

"OK boys, we're here."

Naveed and Jeff came alongside Giant, and they studied the vista. The hills were covered with scattered clusters of trees, brush and rock. A single road wound through, tarmac reflecting the light like a silver river, flowing down towards their small valley-town. Jeff could make out the bright green rectangle of turf that formed the high school football field, home of Giant's distant triumphs, when the two of them had been little more than kids. Jeff was glad that was all history.

"Red-tail," said Giant, pointing to the sky.

Naveed squinted, eventually picking out the shape of a circling hawk.

"Thermalling," Jeff said.

They watched it sail effortlessly on the air, rising higher until it approached the cloud ceiling.

"Will it fly into a cloud?" Naveed spoke their combined thought aloud.

Nobody answered but they all kept their eyes fixed on the tiny speck. A moment before it was due to disappear in white cumulus the bird peeled away and began a slow glide towards a distant peak. With no deviations, it followed a perfectly straight line towards the horizon as though moving along a zipwire.

"It seems to know exactly where it's going," Jeff murmured.

"Wish I could say the same," Nav replied.

"Giant's stuck with you for another year, isn't he?"

Naveed shrugged. "Theoretically, till harvest. I can do analytics remotely."

"You said that last year," Jeff stated. "Something

keeping you here?"

Giant said nothing, wondering where the red-tail had been before, and why it had chosen to climb so high.

Jeff pulled water bottles from his pack. Naveed shook his head, but Giant took one and drank.

"When will we see them?" said Jeff.

"And where?" added Giant.

Naveed glanced at the sun's position, the road, and the town.

"It's hard to be precise, but we could get a few stragglers now. The bulk will come through between two and LOOK!" Naveed's finger stabbed forward, and he swung the gun off his arm.

"Whoa cowboy!" Jeff yelled.

"Never point that at us, remember?" said Giant.

"It's not loaded. You see it?" Naveed said, his voice shrill with excitement.

"It don't matter if you think it ain't loaded. Keep the pointy end down." Jeff stated, deliberately not looking where Naveed was pointing.

"I see it," Giant said, tracking with his finger. "White and blue, four rotors. It's a fast little fucker."

"USPS," Naveed said. "Wouldn't that make it a Federal crime?"

"Tempting," Jeff smiled.

"Let's watch," Giant commanded. They tracked the drone's progress as it briefly paralleled the road before jerking towards the town, where it descended. It became harder to follow, finally disappearing behind a hoarding.

Giant and Jeff held a short conversation on the best hunting position, taking into account a variety of factors that seemed to make a simple task far more complex than Naveed believed was necessary. How hard was it to blow some robotic-insects out of the sky with a double-barrelled shotgun? Naveed had only fired a gun once before, at Giant's farm. Even with his poor aim and fear of a bruised shoulder from the formidable recoil, he'd managed to pick off nearly every skeet Giant had launched into the air.

They strode down the hill to a gathering of rocks with a gnarled tree for shade. Jeff dropped his pack on the ground and cracked open the shotgun to load two cartridges. Naveed copied Jeff's example and could feel his hands sweating. Giant took his time, stretching his back, before gently pulling out his guns. The first was a shotgun with two barrels mounted on top of each other rather than the matrimonial side-by side layout. The second gun resembled a sniper's rifle.

"You know," Giant said, "I used to come here with Amy, before she was dating Jeff. You could see the heat coming off the horizon in waves, but a breeze always flows down the valley to keep you cool. When the leaves turn, and the light comes over Saddle Ridge, the whole valley shines like gold, and the town-lights glitter as though they're jewels." He chuckled to himself.

This was the most Giant had said all day, or for many days. Jeff tried to remember when he'd ever heard him speak like this, when he wasn't drunk. He looked at Naveed, who seemed equally surprised. Giant seemed to have forgotten they were with him.

"Sometimes we'd see deer grazing along the edge of the copse or flicking their heels down the highroad. Once, we saw a puma stretched out in a patch of sunlight, licking his paws, relaxed as a dog by the fire."

A humming-buzz echoed off the hills, like a distant chainsaw. Jeff pulled the gun to his shoulder and swivelled, keeping his red face lifted from the sight as he scanned the sky. Naveed watched for movement, aware that Giant had made no move to collect his weapons.

"My shot," Jeff declared.

Naveed suddenly remembered to pull his plastic ear protectors down in time to muffle the first blast that bounced around the valley and reverberated off the rocks. Naveed saw the drone racing fast to their right, above the tree line. Jeff was tracking it. If he didn't take the shot right now the barrel would be facing Naveed. The second shot exploded in the air before Naveed could duck, and the drone shattered, pieces hurtling in every direction.

"Let's check it out," Giant said.

Naveed propped his gun against a boulder and hopped over the rocks.

"Never leave your gun," Jeff reprimanded him before limping towards the wreckage with his own shotgun slung over his shoulder. Naveed resisted the urge to point out that Jeff's barrels should be pointing down.

Three big pieces of black plastic were lying on open ground. Naveed investigated one piece that resembled a rotor cowling. Jeff had located the more interesting chunk; a brown package with a partial arm of black plastic wrapped around. He waved the package in the air.

"Amazon! Must be for me."

He took a horn-handled knife off his belt and sliced the tape. The box unfolded like the wings of a supercar.

"A book," Jeff said in disgust.

"What were you expecting?" asked Giant.

Jeff furrowed his brow to think of a smart reply, but nothing came. He tossed the book to Naveed.

"Fade to Grey" Naveed said. The others looked blank.

"You know, the sequel or prequel or whatever to Fifty Shades? Porn for housewives."

"It's full of holes," said Jeff, looking at the pellet damage.

"You're probably right about that," Naveed laughed and Giant caught the joke too.

"Who's it for?" Giant asked. "Is there a label?"

"Hey Jeff, perhaps your wife ordered it? Amy doesn't have much to do now your son's at college. What with your knee playing up, eh?"

Giant raised his eyebrows at Naveed from behind Jeff's back and shook his head slightly. Giant needed Naveed's skills to move his family's farm into the modern age. Three generations of farmers, and it could all die with him. Sometimes, he wished he'd taken that football scholarship and simply walked away.

Jeff was busy inspecting the brown box that he'd previously discarded.

"27 El Adobe."

"Corkie's wife, or his daughter," Giant said.

A second buzz came, but Giant called no-shot. "Let's get back in position," he said.

As they walked up the hill they debated ammunition. Giant thought a different shell might destroy the drone without the packages taking collateral damage. Jeff was oblivious. He was more concerned about eliminating as many he could, like a fighter ace chalking kills on his Mustang. While Giant prepared his rifle, slowly and carefully, Jeff took down two more drones. They didn't inspect the remains.

"We can do that later, let's just enjoy this while we can," Jeff said.

Naveed chanced his arm at a couple but only managed to get one shot off before they were overhead. He was surprised how rapidly the drones seemed to approach. Jeff made it look easy.

"I need a taser," Naveed said. "Bust the electrics, then they'd fall out of the sky."

"You've still got to hit it." Jeff said.

Finally, Giant had his rifle in position.

"Not sure this'll work," he said. "The Remington's better for a precision shot, to take something out a long way off."

***

They waited twenty minutes. Two drones flew past, but Giant didn't manage to get a shot as he struggled to adapt the rifle to this new game.

"What was that one?" Jeff asked.

"I think it was Dominos."

"I could eat a pizza. If we see another, I'll take it." Jeff decided.

"Do you like shrapnel in your Hawaiian?" Giant said.

They debated how long it would take before the drones were noticed missing and concluded nobody would do anything until the next day.

"It was beautiful here, before the drone pollution." Giant said, adjusting the sights.

"They should give us a friggin' medal," Jeff said.

"In the future they'll be licenses and a season. The glorious 17th," Naveed declared.

"I thought it was always the 20th?" Jeff asked.

"17 is my lucky number, and your wife's birthday, too," Naveed replied.

"We're out of season," Giant said.

"You were both happy enough to eat Amy's venison

pie, and I shot that out of season," Jeff grumbled.

"She's a good cook, amongst her many talents," Naveed said.

The rifle-shot from Giant caught Jeff and Naveed unawares. There'd been no hum-buzz, and both guys had lifted off their mufflers to talk. Luckily, the rifle was quieter than the shotguns. A splinter of plastic drew a parabola as the trajectory took it to ground, then the drones were overhead, five of them, swarming like wasps around a larger model in the centre.

"You damaged one, " Naveed said.

"What are they?" Giant asked as they swooshed overhead, quiet as an owl's wing.

"Down!" yelled Jeff, and in the next instant he released both barrels from his shotgun in rapid succession, over the heads of his companions. One of the swarm veered to the side and collided with the rising ground on their right, bouncing and careering along until it hit a boulder. Jeff set off to inspect his kill. Bad knee or not he covered the ground quickly with his pack slung over one shoulder and his gun over the other. Giant packed his rifle.

"I'll catch up," he said to Naveed.

Jeff was holding a small black object when Naveed reached him. He held it aloft for Naveed to get a better look. It was a camera, shaped like a bulbous eye.

"What does this look like?" Jeff asked.

"Trouble," Naveed said.

"You know, I shot one of these S-O-Bs down a week ago," Jeff said slowly and deliberately.

"I thought this was the first time. We only agreed to do this because nobody had done it before. If you shot one last week they might have surveillance drones out looking for us, or worse." Colour flushed Naveed's face.

"Hold your horses. I don't mean here. At the grain store, by Alderman's. Damn thing had been stalkin' me. I lured it close and got it comin' round the corner of the barn. Didn't know what hit it."

Giant had arrived. "It was probably that new realtor taking snaps of the buildings."

"I tell yer, it was followin' me."

"Maybe someone wanted to know what you were up to. What *were* you up to Jeff?" Naveed asked.

Jeff spat out his tobacco. "What d'ya mean worse?" he said, taking the conversation a pace back.

Naveed replied with a lowered voice. "You seen the hummingbird clip?"

"Uh-uh," both men shook their heads.

"It's a tiny thing. Flies through windows, navigates stairs, and hunts around until it finds a target using facial recognition. Then POP. Single bullet through the temple."

"Holy crap. Is it real?" Jeff asked.

"People say it's a government device, skunk-works. They're probably using it in North Korea, or on ISIS."

"That's wrong," Giant said.

"Terrorists don't fight clean. I don't see why we should. People get what's comin'," said Jeff, glancing at Naveed.

The familiar low hum caught their attention. Nobody raised a gun, as the appetite for killing had evaporated. Ghosting over the trees came a drone with a strong white light at its heart. It stopped over the area where they'd been standing previously, and the mini-spotlight illuminated an arc for the black spherical eye hanging underneath its belly. The light paused over the spent cartridges. Giant put his finger to his lips with one hand and gestured with the palm of his other hand for them to sink down below the rocks. They shuffled sideways until they were hidden. Giant and Naveed crouched, ready to run. Jeff sat with his legs splayed out in front of him and his back against the rock, gently massaging his upper thigh towards his knee. The drone made an occasional clicking noise. Jeff thought it sounded like a clock ticking in an empty house, while to Naveed it was the sound of a cellphone taking a picture, or a tiny guillotine falling. Giant imagined a casino dealer shuffling cards.

Eventually the drone's hum faded, but nobody moved for a good minute. Giant was the first to check the view, declaring it clear.

"What's the penalty for shooting a drone?" Naveed asked.

"I don't think it's a specific crime yet," Giant said.

"Theft, wilful damage, criminal mischief, anything they feel like. They gotta find us first though. We should make tracks," Jeff said.

"And cover them up," Giant added.

"Glad you too are such criminal masterminds," Naveed jibed.

"Easy enough to dispose of a body out here, if we're talking real crime," Jeff said.

Naveed went pale, but Giant gave a half-laugh and shook his head.

The ridge was looking very exposed with the sun behind it, and any drone with a camera, or even a fool with binoculars, would see them from miles away. Jeff recommended a route that skirted the hill and followed a semi-dry riverbed. It was an extra mile, but they all agreed it was a good option.

The granite riverbed had been absorbing heat all day and was like an oven as they hopped between rocks and crunched across pebbles.

"Godammit," Jeff cursed as he twisted his knee once more. "If I snag this leg Amy will kill me. We're meant to visit her folks this weekend."

"I thought that was off? Amy told me her mom had the flu?" Naveed said.

"You seem to know more about it than me," Jeff said tetchily.

Naveed was holding the gun one-handed, letting it swing as he jumped between stones next to the widening trickle of water down the centre of the riverbed.

"I bumped into her in Starbucks," he said.

Jeff grunted. Stepping close to Naveed, he said quietly by his ear, "You should concentrate on that girl in Bhiri's Store."

Naveed shifted sideways, widening the gap between them.

"What does that mean?" he said.

Jeff put on an easy-going, smooth voice that tried hard to sound relaxed. "I'm jus' saying, it might not be healthy to spend so much time thinkin' about other people's wives."

Naveed wondered if Jeff's shotgun was loaded.

"Here's another," Giant said. "Somebody else took out this doohickey."

Lying in the stream was a drone, partially covered in slime. A camera was visible, along with a covered fan. Giant flipped it over with his foot.

On the side were the letters EPA and a message in a minuscule font, that looked like a warning. Giant bent down to pick it up and the drone flipped from one side to the other, like a stranded fish. Startled, Giant moved back. A yellow light flashed, and the drone flip-flopped again.

"It's alive," Jeff said.

Giant went to stamp on it, and the fan whirred, pushing the drone forward a few feet, until it got caught in shallow water.

"That's not a fan," said Naveed. "It's a propeller."

"It's a friggin' submarine," Jeff declared.

When Giant advanced for the second time, it did three coordinated flips across the ground and sploshed into deeper water on the far side of the pebble island, then began to spin, sending a jet of water into Giant's shirt. He cursed, while the others laughed. A camera flash lit up his face, and then the drone-sub bobbed underwater and accelerated downstream.

"Grab it," yelled Naveed. He jumped into the water, finding it deeper than expected and soaked his jeans up to the knees, which brought him to a stop. Jeff hopped on to a boulder and unleashed both barrels. The surface of the water was peppered, as though handfuls of gravel had been hurled at it, and they looked amongst the patterns for any movement. A ripple ran along the surface away from them, disappearing like the wake of a miniature shark.

"He got a picture for the family album," Giant said.

"Friggin' Environmental Agency insisted they weren't using drones to check for dry run-offs. Then Ackermann got done for dumping manure. Now we know how." Jeff spat.

"At least they won't publish the picture. They want to hide as much as us," Naveed said, making a mental note that Jeff's gun had indeed been loaded.

"I hate drones. Heartless little monsters," Jeff said.

"They're no worse than people," Naveed replied.

"Depends on the person," Jeff said.

"Play nice, boys" Giant said.

***

Following the edge of the riverbed, they headed back towards Jeff's new Chevy. The stream was wider and faster here. Each man tramped forwards in silence, with Giant leading and Naveed close behind, glancing back at Jeff who was limping at the tail of the party.

"This is where we turn," Jeff shouted. The stream tumbled into a waterfall with a shallow pool strewn with boulders about thirty feet below them. On the left, a path twisted around the hillside to where the truck was parked about half a mile away.

"Look," Naveed pointed to the lip of the waterfall. The EPA drone was bobbing in the water, snagged on a branch. The yellow flashing light of earlier was now a constant red. Giant swung the rifle bag off his shoulder to unzip.

"Wait, let me get it," Naveed said.

"Why?" Jeff asked.

"We can stop the photo being used as evidence, for one thing."

"We can do that by blowing it to Kingdom-Come," said Giant as he prepared his rifle.

"If the EPA aren't meant to have them, we might get a payout," Naveed was thinking aloud.

"You're always looking for the angle," Giant mused.

"Or a bigger one if we sell it to a journalist," Jeff said. He looked at the fast-moving water, and the drop to the rocks. "Go for it, Nav," he said.

Naveed looked to Giant for approval, who seemed doubtful.

"Why don't you fetch it?" Giant asked Jeff.

"Naveed's got this," he shrugged. "Unless you want to do it yourself?"

"I'm not the most sure-footed these days," Giant said.

"The bigger they are…" Jeff responded.

The younger man waded out tentatively, keeping a good six-foot from the lip where whitewater disappeared in a crescendo. The water was barely over his knees, but he moved slowly, with arms outstretched like a tightrope walker. Every now and then he wobbled as he struggled to get a foothold. Jeff and Giant watched in silence. When he was opposite the marooned drone, Naveed moved sideways towards the edge, with small steps. Nearing his target, he stretched out his arm.

"Closer," Jeff called.

Naveed took another step and paused to steady himself before reaching for the drone again. This time he got a good hold of the device. He tried to lift it away from the branch, but it was tightly snared.

"Give it a yank," Jeff shouted.

Naveed followed instructions. The drone, the stick, and a large chunk of mud all dislodged at the same time, and the lip crumbled. Naveed lost his footing and slipped into the water, to be pushed over the edge in an instant. He snatched wildly and grasped a protruding root. He was a couple of feet below the top, and it was hard to look because water was cascading down. He struggled, hyperventilating and coughing on water simultaneously. Two black holes with gun-metal irises emerged through the water. Jeff's shotgun.

"Grab a-hold," he heard Jeff yell. Naveed had no option. He could feel the root tearing from the mud wall, and he grabbed the shotgun with his left hand first to make sure it wasn't too slippery and then relinquished his grip on the root to grasp the gun with both hands. Dangling in the air, scrabbling with his feet, he looked directly into the gun barrels.

Jeff was straining to hold the gun and not get pushed over, with the weight of Naveed in front, and the water rushing from behind. Giant waded out into the stream and Jeff twisted his head to see Giant standing behind him. The big man was staring at Jeff's leg, a weak knee at the point of buckling. Any impact there would send Jeff and Naveed tumbling over the edge to the sharp rocks below. Amy would be a widow, with only her old friends for comfort, and a new Chevy made of steel that shone brightly in the sun.

For a second, the scene paused. The three figures held in place like a photograph, framed in that critical instant. It was hard to say how long the scene lasted, but each man measured it differently.

"I'm good with aluminum," Giant said, grabbing Jeff around the waist, and hauling both men upstream.

Reaching the bank, he added, "F150's a fine vehicle. You can't live in the past, no matter how much you'd like to."

"Or the future," said Naveed, coughing-up another mouthful of water.

Jeff lay back to soak up the final rays of sun.

High above, a red-tail called, capturing each man's gaze. Lost in the present, they absorbed its mesmerising spiral ascendance.

When We Were Gone Astray

"What would you like?" the barista asked.

"I'd like the sun to shine," Mark said. The barista nodded, encouragingly. "And my birthday in June, because everyone's in such a bad mood in January."

Now the barista's smile cracked, and Mark flushed red, wondering how he had misread that question so badly.

"That's not what you meant, is it?" Mark said apologetically.

A heavy silence gripped the queue, pressing behind him.

"What would you like?" the barista repeated.

"I'd like a double espresso," and a hole to swallow me up, he thought.

On the road, Mark kept thinking of more things he'd like; ears that stuck out less, and a six-pack to replace his gut; perhaps a superpower like one of the Avengers. Most of all, he wanted a girlfriend like the gorgeous women in the romcom movies which nobody seemed to have noticed.

At the warehouse Mark loaded the deliveries on to his van. The boss dropped snippets of news on the possible takeover and reassured them that their routes wouldn't be affected. The lads dashed off to leave the depot fast, because the sooner they finished the quicker they got home. Mark spotted Tim the Aussie performing a final check of his consignments, and he looked slightly lost — as though he were waiting for something, an interaction, a conversation, before heading out. Mark thought the other drivers paid less attention to Tim because he was not a local. Maybe that's why Tim always lingered, looking for a word or two — just to feel seen. Mark knew the feeling.

"Question for you," Mark said to start a conversation. "What super-power would you like?"

"Easy one," Tim laughed. "I'd like to be lucky."

"Is that all?" Mark said.

"Luck. What else do you need mate?"

"I don't know, teleportation? Psychic powers?" Mark stuttered.

Tim smiled. "What would you do with them? Keep it simple."

"I guess so. Nothing else?"

"Well," Tim looked thoughtful, "I guess invisibility might be handy when the wife is looking for some help with the dishes," he winked.

Mark climbed into his vehicle and let the engine warm the cabin. The more he thought about it, the more it seemed Tim was right. Luck was the missing ingredient in his life, the element that would make everything good again. He crossed his fingers and knocked on the fake walnut dash.

***

Donna Wiśniewski drifted through the shopping mall, slower than the rushing early-birds, as she was in no hurry to arrive at work. The crowd parted and flowed around her, but she caught the sideways glances, often curious, and a little judgemental. At six-foot-two in her navy-blue nurse's uniform, blending in was impossible, even though she tried. Her last name tangled the local tongues into knots, and she had adopted the name Donna as a disguise, an easier, friendlier starting point that acted as a soft shield against the discomfort of standing out.

Today was Friday, which meant a caramel macchiato

from the café, sipped slowly while wandering past shops that were still closed this early. The displays were decked with baubles and tinsel, and a veritable plague of miniature silver deer. Donna had her eye on a Katie Cuthbert bag. Every morning she gazed at it through the shop-window, the rose-patterned material shining like summers past. The bag was a tangible reminder of happiness, just out of reach. She calculated that by resisting her coffee she could afford the bag in twenty-two weeks. That was never going to happen. She wished there was someone who would buy it for her. It was a shame the mall didn't have stores that sold lovers, with warranties, user-guides, and guarantees of satisfaction. None of her past relationships had come with such assurances, that was for sure. It always seemed to be her that tried to fix stuff, to patch things up, to give more than she got. Donna thought she could write the manual on quiet disappointment, and bad luck, but who would want to buy that? She headed towards the bus stop, trying not to make too much noise with her large feet that she'd been told were loud when she walked. It was much colder than she'd realised, and she didn't have a coat. If she were lucky, the bus would be along in a few minutes.

Inside Talbot Ward the Staff Nurse pressed the door release button, and Donna walked in stiffly.

"You look white as a fish-belly," she said to Donna.

"Late bus."

One of the patients moved precariously towards her and the Staff Nurse.

"Ooh dear, you look frozen. Can I get you a hot drink?" the old woman said.

"Thank you, Molly, I'm fine," Donna said.

"It's no trouble. The kitchen's right there," she pointed to the exit.

"Why don't we see who's here today?" Donna said guiding her gently away from the triple-locked door. Donna said hello to the six patients lined in hard plastic chairs along the back wall. They stared at the TV but gave no sign of interest or enjoyment. At a certain stage of decline the patients could no longer follow language, as everybody spoke too quickly for them. As an immigrant, she found it easy to sympathise.

After settling Molly in a chair next to another friendly chatterbox, Donna went to tidy each bedroom. A stuffed sock-dog sat on a bedside cabinet in room 114, gazing at Donna as she scooped soiled clothes off the floor.

"I'm going to live for every moment," she said. The stuffed sock-dog stared back, but he kept his thoughts private.

"At least somebody loved you," she told him.

She tucked the sheets in. "All I want is what you've had. I'm not fussy. He doesn't even have to be taller than me." Not many men were, she thought. "But he has to be a little bigger than you," she said, in case the sock-dog had the wrong idea.

After breakfast was cleared away, the first family members began arriving for visits. Very few came more than once a week and some far less. The burden of pain was too much. New patients could get emotional if nobody visited them, and Donna pretended to handle paperwork while she kept an eye on them.

Donna saw some puzzled faces at the door. New visitors. She pressed the release button by the desk and fished out a tissue for a man the Staff Nurse was consoling. She could see Molly approaching the visitors. For an old lady, she was surprisingly fast. The younger man wore the panicked look of a first-time visitor, that primary horror of being trapped in the asylum. Donna gently shepherded Molly away, before returning to help the visitors. The young man held a bunch of pink roses.

"Those look lovely," Donna said, half-wishing they were for her.

"It's my parent's Wedding Anniversary. Do you have a vase?"

"That's really nice, but I'm not sure we have any," she said.

He looked surprised.

"We don't allow flowers here," Donna added, "The patients eat them."

***

Mark banged hard on the door. He could hear the dogs going wild but nobody else was stirring. He'd met the dogs before. He was cool with them. He liked the idea of owning a dog — someone waiting in the flat when he got home, always pleased to see him. It wasn't practical though, with him on the delivery-round all day. He gave one more knock for good luck then ticked the boxes on his WhileYouWereOut card, slipping it through the letterbox and making sure not to poke his fingers through. All the drivers knew enough horror stories about dogs and didn't take risks. This was his sixth delivery without finding a person at home. No interactions, no chance for a conversation or a connection. He jumped back in the cab. The radio debate for the morning was on elderly care. Caller after caller explained how their relative had been ill-treated or robbed. He couldn't believe how cruel the world had become. Having swallowed his measure of misery for one day, he switched to a music channel, flicking through stations until he recognised a tune. He glanced at his schedule. Five more deliveries before lunch.

***

Donna brandished the vase like a trophy.

"You found one," the young visitor said, sitting with his parents.

"Beauty!" said the visitor's mother.

"Shall I put them in your room?"

"Yes, yes, beauty."

"Just this once, OK?" she confirmed with the men. "No more flowers."

The visitor passed the bouquet to Donna and she walked down the corridor to room 121. With the vase in one hand, she tucked the flowers under her arm and awkwardly used the key tied to her waist to open the door. They had to keep bedrooms locked because the patients wandered, taking items and sleeping wherever and whenever they could. There was a sink inside and she half-filled the vase with water. An elastic band held the roses together and she unhooked them. She knew you were meant to snip a few centimetres off the bottom of the stems, but scissors were also banned on Talbot Ward. A small plastic packet of plant food fell out of the rose packaging. She bent down to scoop it up and saw a bulge under the mattress. Busy with the task in hand she tore at the tough plastic package with her teeth, trying not to get a mouthful of plant food. A single drop of sweet sugar-water kissed her lip, and she poured the rest into the vase and carefully arranged the roses to leave them spreading colour on the bedside table.

Lifting the mattress with one hand Donna groped underneath with the other until she found and grasped the lump. Even the most common princess would feel that huge pea under her bed. Pulling it out, she let the mattress fall back into place. She stared at the tightly bundled wad of fifty-pound notes and thought of the Katie Cuthbert bag.

***

With his shift finished, Mark wandered through the mall. He had a Christmas list on a scrap of paper torn from his delivery pad. It read *Mum*, with a question mark next to her name, and *Mrs Cooper*, with chocolates scrawled beside her name. She was his neighbour and took deliveries for Mark when he was out making deliveries. On a whim, he purchased a bottle of brandy to keep himself warm in the winter nights, along with the chocolates for Mrs Cooper, all at the department store. It took forever to queue and pay. He had no idea what to get his mum and was flustered by people bustling past. Pausing for a moment to listen to the carol singers, he hummed along to God rest ye merry gentlemen, when a bright display caught his attention. He saw a bag, pale green and covered with a tiny rose-motif. He moved closer and squinted through the window to see the price tag.

***

Donna stopped briefly to listen to the choir in the mall's atrium. It was one of her favourite carols and she mouthed the words, too shy to join in.

"God rest ye merry gentlemen, let nothing you dismay, for Jesus Christ our Saviour was born on Christmas day, to save us all from Satan's power, when we were gone astray…"

She walked towards the Katie Cuthbert store, humming the melody. Donna glanced through the glass to see the bag was gone. Her head remained fixed on the vacant space where her dreams had settled, as her legs carried her forward like an automaton. She slammed into a man coming out of the shop. A plastic bag spun from his hand and the sound of glass shattering echoed throughout the hall, as the bag hit the marble floor.

Donna swore in Polish. Mark looked at the smashed

debris. Everyone froze to stare at the commotion, and Mark could feel all eyes of the crowd on them, waiting to see and judge his response. He hated being the centre of attention and could feel colour rising up his neck. Ignoring the crowd, Mark looked at the woman. She was the same height as him, which was rare, but suited her. She had striking dark eyes offset by shiny hair tied scruffily at the back, and he got the sensation that she was thoughtful, although he couldn't quite say why. She wore a uniform but so did he. Her navy-blue outfit was more attractive than his brown jumpsuit. He thought her face was kind. His initial reaction was to swear too, but he held his tongue. He wondered how you could tell the difference between good and bad luck.

"Are you alright?" He asked and reached his arm out towards her.

Donna saw the man had the Katie Cuthbert bag nestled under the other arm. Her dream bag, wrapped delicately in pink tissue paper, destined for someone else's happiness. She was angry, disappointed, and exhausted. The man was waiting patiently for her to respond. Her cheeks burned, and she looked into the man's eyes as he waited — for what? An apology? A connection? Money?

"Clumsy oaf," she said, and turned away.

His eyes were gentle, she thought, but Donna gripped her empty purse tightly and dared not look back as she briskly marched into the distance, while the crowd parted but continued to stare at her with its many judgemental eyes. There was no sound of pursuit, and Donna was shocked to find tears running down her cheek. The realisation came to her that the anger was not directed at the man. With every step she took away from the scene, she felt more hollow. Just as the broken bottle spilled its amber contents over the marble floor, her dreams were leaking away.

***

Mark watched the woman disappearing into the mall, her head held high, and saw her shoulders slump, recognising how hard she was trying to hold herself together. Sometimes, he walked that way in the warehouse, relaxing only when he slid into the cab of his vehicle. He prepared to call out, to let her know it was all OK, but the words stuck in his throat. He could feel the crowd's hostility towards her, and thought it was better to let her make an escape. Mark stooped to rescue the chocolates, and an attendant arrived to sweep away the smashed pieces of glass. He told Mark the department store might give him a replacement, if he was lucky. Mark thanked the attendant and headed towards his van instead. He replayed the moment, wondering if he'd said the wrong thing, or if he should have said nothing, and whether it even mattered. Maybe this was how luck worked, it was slippery, hard to catch, and he just didn't have the knack. He put his purchase in the vehicle and hesitated. He could buy a bottle at the supermarket on the way home but that would be crazily busy, and it would cost him. The attendant was right — the department store might give him a replacement. It was worth a try.

***

Donna wiped her eyes in the café queue and hoped her mascara hadn't run. Opening her purse, she counted the small change that remained, just enough for a filter coffee.

"What would you like?" the barista asked.

Thoughts of coffee evaporated.

"A time-machine," Donna said. She wasn't thinking of dinosaurs or the Last Supper, just a chance to undo her blunders.

"Sorry?" The barista said.

Donna considered that a time-machine was simply a tool that took you to places where you could fix mistakes. If you only travelled to witness events, you might as well watch a movie or read a history book. Donna looked at her oversized feet. Maybe she already owned a time-machine. It just took courage to use it. The queue and the barista were running out of patience.

"What-do-you-want?" the barista said slowly, as though talking to an idiot.

"The simplest things," Donna said softly. She walked out of the store and into the mall, where she approached the cleaner mopping the floor outside Katie Cuthbert. It was ridiculous, wasn't it, to think this could be fixed? She hesitated, but she'd already wasted so much time going nowhere. She forced herself to move on.

After thanking the cleaner, Donna's large feet transported her towards the department store. There had been many times where she wished to be as wealthy as some of her patients, but as Donna walked over the marble slabs it was clear to her that time was a far more valuable currency than money. The roll of cash from her patient's bed was safely locked away in the hospital safe, where she had deposited it, even though the owner had no more use for little bits of green paper. There are many times, she thought, where money has no meaning. She could apologise to the man with an open heart, even if she could not repay him from her empty purse. She didn't know why the man in brown had bought the Katie Cuthbert bag, but she did know it was dangerous to live on assumptions.

In the Customer Service queue of the department store, she saw the man, waiting patiently. He was chatting to an older woman behind him in the queue and what looked like her grandchild, making them both laugh. Donna faltered. She could still turn back, and avoid the risk of rejection or anger, but wasn't that what she always did? Donna took a deep breath. This wasn't about the bag or money, it was about taking a step forward into the kind of life she wanted to create, the person she was determined to become. Donna smiled nervously, prepared an apology, and let her size-eleven time-machine carry her into a future with brighter days, and maybe a few real roses waiting to bloom.

Race For The Pot

I found a lump today, while I was at work. If I slip two fingers between my shirt buttons, I can feel a swelling beneath the skin, bigger than a coin. It's firm and not particularly squidgy, although I haven't had the courage to push too hard. Everyone knows that a lump means cancer. The sooner you get it treated, they say, the higher your chance of survival. I should go to the doctor, but my philosophy has always been that it's better to live in hope than face a harsh and hostile truth. Plus, I'm scared-to-death of doctors and I've much bigger problems — the dean will kill me if I don't find him four lobsters in the next two hours.

I walk through the inner quad. Sunlight pours through the branches of the gigantic elm tree, and I pause in the cloisters and watch light spilling over its leaves in a cascade of blues. I think about my sister who is deeply religious, she would tell me to have faith. While we share a sense of humour, our world view is very different. I consider the number of times I've stopped to look at this elm tree in its various moods, branches tearing holes in the mist, or late summer rays setting the crimson leaves alight. The pagans worshipped dryads, picked omens from the arc of a swallow's flight or the wistful hoot of an owl. They grasped for meaning in nature's beauty. If I had a religion, that might be mine. I listen carefully to see what advice the elm might offer in my hour of need, but it whispers too quietly, while the diffused cobalt light swirls around me. I turn, knock on a wooden panel, and step out of this sanctuary into the narrow lane.

The gargoyles leer at me from the roof. I pass a cluster of ultra-polite Japanese tourists. They are crouching, cameras on mini-tripods with tilting heads gawking at the grotesques. For some superstitious reason, I avoid treading on their shadows, in case my bad luck is contagious.

I could have sent Andy or Steve on this shellfish errand, but the lump has made me restless. I need to meander in the hope that life may rediscover me. There's nobody in the present who I would trust with my news, who wouldn't find it a burden. I would rather stumble across a ghost from my past. With the right person, I could find deliverance. We could wander through shadowed streets and talk of the dreams we cling to, no matter how faded or tattered they seem.

The city wall curls away from me, and the honeyed stone feels rough against my palm. The sky is sharp blue, and the sunlight cuts, slicing the road as it slashes through gaps in the buildings. I walk on and realise it's too bright for ghosts. The past has gone, leaving me marooned in the here and now, with no bridge to the future.

Dinner is only a few hours away and I need to get those damned lobsters that the dean foolishly promised his guests. He never checks with us first. I think he does it deliberately, testing me, to prove my lack of value — a man of no degree.

I walk past Radcliffe Camera. The building is encircled by iron spikes that keep foreigners and locals a safe distance from the rarefied intellectuals within. Gathered outside the Camera is a group of laughing students in their late teens. They block my way, but not deliberately. They seem unaware of anyone or anything other than their tight-knit group. I vividly remember being that age; hammering out rhythms on cedar-faced guitars, picnicking on fresh figs, seeing love reflected by a pair of earth-coloured eyes, long since lost. I ponder whether my life consists of an allocated number of months, a tally of heartbeats, or if it would be better measured in memories?

Inside the Covered Market, I pass the cheese counter.

I have no appetite. A young customer orders a wedge of Oxford Blue as I pass by. Hooked outside the butcher's is a hind, a brace of pheasant, and the delivery bike, high enough to stay out of reach of all but the most athletic students. A few more steps and I reach the fishmongers. In the queue, I can't resist the urge to slip a finger between my shirt buttons and circle the lump. I've been vaguely aware of it for at least a month. Sliding into bed late at night, I've sensed a fault, like that annoying rattle in the car that you only notice when a passenger makes a passing comment. The fishmongers have nothing left but ice and whitebait, plus one sad looking salmon, slit from neck-to-tail. I gesture to Billy, the owner.

"Lobster?" I say.

He shakes his head. "Four am tomorrow. You want me to hold some?"

"Nothing in the freezer?" I ask.

"Sorry, mate."

I lurk by the designer cake shop and consider my next move. Sugary brides and grooms dance on violins and parachute over cakes. There's an impressive model of Christ Church college with a crowd of marzipan guests.

"Marvellous," an American lady says, admiring the confectionary.

"You know," I say, "that all food kills you?"

"Everything kills you in excess," she replies, tapping her fingernails on the window.

"Food is a murderer, even in moderation. We're like cars. You have to use fuel to power the car, but the little impurities and particles eventually clog the engine."

"Like salt?"

"One day salt is the killer, and red wine is healthy. The next day they switch roles, because all food types have a lethal capacity as well as a benefit."

"Salt is always bad," she says.

"So why do they use saline drips at the hospital?" I ask. She concedes the point, and I continue. "You need food, but it blocks the arteries, fills the brain with heavy metals, thins the skin, and wears you down."

The woman is wearing a white dress with a subtle blue pattern that reminds me of the scattered light from the elm tree.

"How do you know all this?"

"I'm a chef," I say.

"Ahhh," she smiles. "Then what should I eat?"

"Anything you want. We all die so you might as well enjoy yourself."

"Fascinating. I'm no expert, but I have found that sometimes your theory is reversed — food can save your life. A pleasure to meet you."

She holds my hand tightly, not releasing it until she has finished, marking the end of our dialogue. Staring at her reflection in the shop window as she walks away, I see the candy college and I know where to try next, Christ Church. They're sure to have a few lobsters, and the master-chef is a good guy. As I rush out of the Covered Market, I pass the jewellers, where every watch seems to be counting down time, just for me.

***

The porter at the college doesn't recognise me, so I flash my ID, but he's busy with a group of Spanish teachers and their unruly mob. Eventually I get through, and head to the kitchen. The master-chef's missing, although I'm told he'll be back in five, so I wander into the cathedral. I don't normally do tourist-stuff. A grey-haired helper wobbles over, unsteadily.

"That's the white rabbit's door," he says, pointing across a grassy area to a wall with a small door in the middle. "Charles Dodgson wrote Alice here. Those were his rooms, and when pursued by a student he would dash back, slipping through there. The inspiration for the white rabbit's door."

"I'm late," I say.

The helper-guide is about to launch into a lecture. I quickly thank him and move deeper into the cathedral. There's a tomb in one corner, covered in stone ivy with peeping faces. Oxford is one of those places where history is deeply layered, no matter how ancient something appears, there's always something older buried inside. Overlooking the sarcophagus is an intricately carved wooden balcony, its steps worn away by thousands of worshippers. The sign states that this was the shrine of Saint Frideswide, built in 1289 to hold the relics of a Saxon lady who lived 700 years before the college was formed. I touch the carvings, and caress one of her many stone faces. Light enters through a stained glass, highlighting her smiling face in pale blue, dust motes swirling in the beams.

Ten minutes later I'm walking through the meadow, with a heavy bag of ice containing four live lobsters. It's hotter now, and the bag is dripping. I can feel the lobsters squirming. Strictly speaking, the creatures should be frozen for two hours to render them unconscious. Then we use a skewer to pierce the cross on their heads, conveniently placed to allow chefs to perform instant executions. That's current best practice for the humane preparation of shellfish. I don't have two hours. We'll need to handle this the old-fashioned way. The dean may be a stickler for ethics, but people don't get slowly numbed and terminated, we must face our exit, however and whenever it appears. If that's good enough for people, it should be fine for lobsters.

***

Our names are stacked under four spice jars with coloured lids, each matching the spot of colour we've dabbed on a lobster. One of them has a mis-shaped shell, and I daubed that one in blue, and set my name against it. Andy holds two and Steve has the yellow one lined up. They have ten feet to cover from table legs to the cooker, where the water is boiling furiously. Race for the pot.

"Are you ready?" I ask. Andy and Steve both assent, and one lobster clacks its claws on the floor.

"On your marks," I say.

If Blue wins, I tell myself, everything will be fine. My lump will be a minor issue that fades, a cyst maybe, something benign. I don't know why this thought occurs to me, but somehow, I completely believe it's true. My fate will be settled in the next sixty seconds. For some reason, I picture the elm tree filling the courtyard, sighing and shivering in the cooling air, stirring to take its part in the process.

"Go!" I shout.

Andy and Steve release their captives. There's no movement at first, as though the lobsters can't believe they're free. Yellow turns around, and Steve repositions him to face forward. Andy prods Green and Red takes the early lead, but Blue is in pursuit, and when Red pauses, Blue clambers on top of him, unsure whether to fight or mate. Green has started slowly but seems to be heading steadily for the pot in a determined fashion.

"Come on Blue" I say.

Andy and Steve encourage their chosen bets. Green keeps moving forward.

"Bluey. Come on Blue. You can do it."

It's crazy, I know. The fate of this armoured crustacean can't possibly have anything to do with my life, but now I've made the connection I can't break it.

"Bluey! Move it!" I start to swear. My voice rises in volume. Andy and Steve fall silent.

"Blue, Blue, Blue." I'm screaming, and I realise everyone has stopped, except Blue who is moving again. He cuts diagonally across the route, possibly to intercept Green. I yell at him. I see the dean's feet, shuffling forward. I glance at him, and his boiled-red face, then at the sheepish expressions of my assistants, but it's too late now. Bluey gets one claw across the finish line. I snatch him up and drop him in the pan. The dean yells, spitting fury. He moves towards the stove, and I block his way. I don't really hear his words. I do hear the water bubbling, and as it sank, I was distinctly aware of the sacrificial hiss made by the blue lobster's shell. My attention is captured by the light that penetrates the window, filtering through the elm tree. The light is golden now, warm and encompassing. I smile at the dean as he rants and rages. Everything will be okay.

This Is Not How It Ends

They gathered a few feet from the edge and shuffled forwards. Alan leaned out for a better view, intensely aware of the jostling group behind him. Beyond a crumbling lip of limestone, the world was made of turquoise and light. A seagull swerved into view, and the sudden movement and revealed depth made Alan recoil. They were all going to dive into the water twenty metres below, and Alan was going first. The instructor clapped his hands.

"OK people, gather round. Let's not freak out before we've started."

The instructor was a muscular powerhouse towering above the teenagers. His Mexican assistant was closer to Alan's size but with a torso from the cover of a health magazine. The instructor continued. "You all know the routine. Nobody would be here if they didn't have the technique."

A ripple of laughter came from a mumbled comment at the back, but Alan missed the joke. His mouth was dry.

"Sanchez will demonstrate one last time. That means he'll be in the water as you dive. When you surface remember to swim to Sanchez and not bob around waiting for a human missile to land on you."

Alan tried to stay focused. He suddenly couldn't remember how he'd got here. The whole summer seemed a blur of practice sessions in the pool. There had been dancing, laughter and Monica; with brunette hair tied back her face was a perfectly shaped frame for those horizon-blue eyes. She glanced at him now. They didn't talk much. He found the words hard and never seemed to get it right.

"Alan, come here so you can see this," the instructor

said. "Remember, number one. The step-up." Sanchez demonstrated by walking forward to the red marker.

"Two, spread your wings," the instructor said, and Sanchez pushed his shoulders back, flexed his neck and then deliberately moved his arms like a bird about to take flight.

"Three, the arrow," Sanchez raised his arms above his head to make a steeple.

"Go."

Springing from his heels Sanchez vanished faster than Icarus. The cluster of teenagers held their breath, until one girl on the edge pointed.

"There!" she shouted.

The crowd cheered and Sanchez waved in an exaggerated fashion before swimming towards the overhang and disappearing from view.

"It's not rocket science ladies and gentlemen." The instructor slapped Alan heartily on the shoulder. "Alan, show us what you can do."

Alan had planned to wink at Monica, but it was taking all his effort just to walk. The instructor spoke softly so that only Alan could hear. "Follow the steps. It'll be swell," he said. This last word sounded false in the instructor's mouth. It was one of *their* words. He hated it when they tried to sound hip.

"One," the instructor barked.

Alan took three paces to the marker and placed his feet precisely on the line. He swallowed mouthfuls of salt-air as commands two and three followed rapidly. Alan's arms were raised above his head but weighed-down like lead, and he felt precariously unbalanced. There was no sound but the wet slap of the ocean's giant hands.

"Go!"

Conditioning caused him to leap. All he could see was a palette of turquoise and azure. For a moment, he felt suspended in the air, lighter than a feather, followed by a rush of adrenalin, then a white explosion. Disorientated, he kicked towards the light, groping with his hands until he burst through the ocean's skin. The sun reflected off the water, blinding him with fragments of gold. Sanchez was at his side.

"Well done," he said and Alan waved wildly to an audience he couldn't see.

"Let's go," Sanchez swam and Alan followed until they reached a boulder protruding from the sea like a giant turtle's back, Sanchez offered a hand and pulled him from the water.

"It was good, no?" Sanchez asked.

"Swell."

On the cliff, Monica watched the others take their place in line, then leap off like obedient lemmings. She was relieved Alan had made it safely. Monica felt queasy. It wasn't the idea of the dive itself but fear of making a mistake. She didn't want to let anyone down. Monica lacked confidence with physical tasks, but they'd been through the routine so many times that she was expected to have it memorised.

"You're next Monica." The instructor held her hand, squeezing it gently before she stepped into position.

"One."

She walked to the line.

"Two."

Monica held her arms out to the side, like Christ on a Crucifix.

"Three."

She formed the steeple.

"Go."

Confused, she stepped forward instead of jumping and slipped over the edge. Smashing, tumbling, her arms flailing, she called out in terror as she thrashed. She felt a sharp pain tear her left arm as she spun into the darkening aquamarine.

Below, the turtle-boulder was squeezed tight with teenagers. Alan had been shivering as he watched the last few divers, waiting patiently for Monica. They heard her scream. The waterproof walkie-talkie of Sanchez buzzed with static.

"EMT," it said as a body pirouetted into the water with a plume of spray.

"The green toggle," Sanchez shouted. "Pull your green toggle."

Ken went pop like a balloon, then Ray and two others standing beside him. Like bubblewrap the teenagers vanished with a loud snap as they yanked the green toggles attached to their trunks.

"You too, Alan."

He clasped it between his knuckles and pulled sharply, as on the cord of a lawnmower. There was an unpleasant sensation like a paper bag bursting in his head. He lay still for a moment, feeling his heart race. He breathed deeply before slowly opening his eyes.

A hospital ward. Blinding light from the windows. A thin blue sheet covering him. His bed made from pipes. Alan let his hand explore the tubes raised either side of him like a cot. Opposite were two beds containing old men. Alan noticed a girl sitting in a chair to his right, looking intently at him.

"Grandad?" the girl said.

"Hello," Alan replied, clearing his throat.

"It's me. Rachel," she said.

"Hello Rachel. I must have been dreaming."

"No you were in VEEP," Rachel said. "Do you remember what that stands for?"

"No, I don't."

"It's a place they take you to recover," she said.

"Am I ill?" Alan asked.

"You had a stroke. Remember? Two months ago."

"No," Alan said. "I don't remember."

"Your neighbour found you. He called an ambulance and the police. They had to break down your door," Rachel told him.

"So where am I?"

Rachel smiled and Alan suspected he must have asked that many times before. "You're in Victoria Hospital in Blackpool."

"Am I getting better?" Alan asked.

"You're making good progress physically."

It seemed a slippery answer but Alan didn't want to ask the follow-on question, and Rachel showed no inclination to say any more.

"How old am I?" Alan asked.

"You're eighty-five."

"I thought I was seventeen."

"Well, you were once," she smiled, gently.

"That's really old," Alan said with feeling. "There was an accident, for Monica." he added.

"Grandma?" asked Rachel. "Wait here. I'll be back in a minute."

"I'm not going anywhere," Alan said, but Rachel had already gone.

Alan studied his swollen hands. There were bruises on his wrists and forearms and the skin was textured with hundreds of tiny, permanent wrinkles. Only a minute ago he'd been a teenager plummeting into the sea, and now he was an old man with a twenty-something grandchild. His head throbbed trying to piece the puzzle together. He closed his eyes to think.

**

Alan woke uneasily. He was on a minibus that rattled and shook. It was dark outside, although a pink tinge through the windscreen suggested it was sunrise. Sanchez was driving and the instructor was alongside him. Alan looked at his hands. They were slim with tanned skin stretched tight over agile fingers. He wiggled his fingers and turned his hands over to admire their perfection. Monica was next to him. There was something puzzling about her being there, some incident half-remembered.

He looked up to find the instructor standing over him, stooped to avoid the low roof. He was studying Alan, thinking with his eyes. Alan opened his mouth to ask a question but wasn't sure what to say.

"Monica's fine, Alan. She hurt her arm last week but she's alright now."

"OK," Alan said and felt better. Today, he would ask her on a date.

The sun was yawning into a washed-out sky when they arrived. Monica stirred as they lurched to a full stop.

"We're here," Alan told her.

"Where?" she said dreamily.

"Here." Alan wasn't entirely sure of the answer.

The instructor had them gather in a circle.

"Today's activity is rock-climbing," he said. "We're going to have a picnic up there." The instructor pointed to a rock-wall and slowly raised his hand until they were staring at the sky, where the rock was brushing against a cloud.

"Jump off a cliff one day, climb it the next," Alan whispered to Monica. "I wish they'd make their bloody minds up."

Sanchez showed them the complex sequence of loops

they needed to make the rope knot. Monica did hers without too much trouble, but Alan found it hard, even with his nimble fingers. Monica did it for him.

Sanchez went first, free climbing. A minute later the first rope uncoiled down the cliff, dangling like a brightly coloured snake.

"It's not a race," the instructor said. "Take your time and always keep three points anchored. We'll get into dynamic moves another day."

Alan leaned back in his harness and watched Monica swiftly climb the rock face. She was confident and made it look easier than walking up stairs. It wasn't a race, but Alan saw that Monica was first to the top. Now it was his turn.

After a few minutes climbing he began to tire and realised he was stuck. Where the holds had seemed large and plentiful, now they were small and awkward. He felt for another hold with his left foot. His right toes remained precariously perched on a narrow ledge and his fingers ached as they squeezed together to grip the small holds sustaining him. His groping foot could find nothing. He brought it back to the last ledge where it had held purchase. Alan's left leg began to jerk up and down uncontrollably. Fear punched into his stomach. He told himself the rope would hold. He'd watched Monica tie the knot, but wasn't the left loop meant to go through the right, and hadn't she done it vice versa? As easily as a spider on a thread, Sanchez slid into place next to him.

"OK Alan, there's a foothold just here," he tapped the rock with his toe to indicate the spot. "Then move your other foot here," he tapped another spot with his hand this time. "Only a few feet left."

Having Sanchez next to him was the impetus he needed and suddenly there was Monica reaching out to pull him over the top. She hugged him tight with relief and love,

Alan thought, definitely love.

Sanchez herded them towards the woven picnic rugs and Alan felt good. Everybody was exhilarated and they sang together, an impromptu concert with tunes that everyone knows.

"Monica," Alan said, and she turned her eyes on him. "Would you like, I mean perhaps one evening…"

"Yes," she said, and he wasn't sure if it was a question or a confirmation but it gave him the confidence to finish his sentence.

"…we could see the city lights? They're beautiful from the Giant's Kitchen."

"I'd love to," she said.

The instructor announced a surprise.

"We're going home via a shortcut." He held up a backpack with various straps hanging off it. "This is a rapid deployment parachute. You're going to enjoy this!"

Alan and Monica stood hand-in-hand about twenty-foot from the cliff edge. Alan's heart was thumping, and Monica's hand gripped his like a vice. The instructor made them both repeat the instructions and then gave a thumbs-up. They ran forwards and hurled themselves off the edge. It was spectacular. This was the life he had always hoped for. Who could ask for more?

"Pull," Alan shouted.

He tore at the green ripcord and saw Monica do the same thing. They were jolted apart, and he felt a pop as the parachute opened.

***

"Dad, can you hear me?"

Alan opened his eyes. His hand grabbed the tube-side

of his bed and ran along the smooth aluminium. He looked to his side and sitting in the chair was a middle-aged woman with Monica-coloured eyes.

"Was I asleep?" Alan said.

"You've just woken up. It's Stephanie."

"Where am I Stephanie?"

"Victoria Hospital. You had a stroke."

"But I'm getting better."

"That's good," Stephanie said.

A rotund male nurse came into the room. Alan noticed his name badge said Sanchez. He checked Alan's drip and made a note on his clipboard. Stephanie asked Sanchez a question that Alan missed.

"It is safe," Sanchez replied in a thick accent.

"Look at the bruises on his arm," Stephanie said.

Alan lifted his arm to inspect the purple patterns for himself.

"Alan forgets he is attached to a drip. He goes walkabout and it detaches. We must find a new insertion. You remember the drip, uh Alan?" Sanchez said.

"My Mum's arms are worse," Stephanie said.

Sanchez answered. "Yes, she wave her arms after a bad VEEP, and collide her bed. Skin is very thin. It bruises like, a plum? VEEP is safe though."

Stephanie seemed agitated to Alan. The conversation was making little sense to him because they talked so fast.

"Are there statistics, evidence of the results?" Stephanie said and Sanchez nodded, used to dealing with such requests.

"VEEP is proven to accelerate physical and mental recuperation for ischemia strokes in both primary degenerative and vascular dementia. I give you URL?"

"That would be helpful," Stephanie said, partially

appeased.

Sanchez was not finished. "We use VEEP to enhance the quality of life, for pleasure to people with limited mobility or memory functions."

"I'm not sure I see how," Stephanie said.

"It provides dignity and a graceful..." Sanchez paused to search for the right words, "celebration of life."

"Is that really God's way?" Stephanie asked.

"I can't answer for him, but it is our way."

Rachel entered the room, hesitantly.

"Hi Grandad. How are you feeling?"

"Not too bad," Alan said. "Bed fourteen," he pointed to the old man opposite.

"Yes, and you're in bed seventeen."

Alan counted round the beds like the numbers on a clock, "And your Grandma is in bed..." he let the sentence hang.

"Thirty-two," Rachel said.

"That's right," Alan nodded as though he'd known all along.

Sanchez came and mixed some powder into Alan's orange juice to thicken it and gave him a spoon. Alan kept repeating the number thirty-two. Eventually his eyes fell shut. When he opened them next it was dark. He pulled himself upright and slid his feet into the worn slippers by his bedside. He collected a bag from the bedside cabinet and clutched it tightly. Then he walked unsteadily towards the corridor. There was a ping as his drip pulled out of his arm.

At each bay, he studied the numerals. Eventually he found bed thirty-two. Monica was still awake. Alan put a finger to his lips.

"Put these on," he said and handed her the bag.

"19 Rigby Lane, Bolton," Monica said.

"Give me five minutes," Alan said and shuffled away.

"Don't be late!" Monica shout-whispered, and then laughed until she coughed.

Back at his bed Alan took a second pair of goggles and slipped them on.

His Norton rumbled as it burbled past the terraced houses at a walking pace. Monica was already standing outside her house. She wore a floral green dress, and her hair was tied back with a bow.

"You look fabulous! Hop on." Alan shouted above the growling engine. Monica straddled the motorbike and held his waist one hand on either side, rather than all the way around the middle.

"Let's go," she said.

He kept the engine low until they'd navigated out of town. Once they reached the hills he opened the throttle wide and the Norton roared into the evening. He flipped the bike left then right to cope with the switchbacks, and as they climbed higher Alan felt like an eagle rising into the sky on a thermal, gazing at the glittering world spread below.

There was a bench at the top and they sat cuddled together, Alan's arm around her shoulders as they looked at the twinkling lights.

"Did we do this before?" Alan asked.

"No, you only had a scooter."

"That's right," he said. "We should have done it."

"We were always too busy, with work, then the kids. There was never enough time for us."

"There are moments when everything comes back into focus. The scooter, the holidays, all of it seems real again," Alan said, and Monica leaned into him. "I think it's time we planned one last journey," he said.

"Yes," Monica murmured, "I was thinking that. Let me

pick you up in my Triumph Stag. We didn't have one of those either, but I always wanted a yellow one."

***

Alan opened his eyes to the dazzling sunlight streaming through the window.

"Morning Grandad," a female voice. Alan turned to find a young woman sitting by his bed. She was familiar, and he thought long and hard before he said her name.

"Rachel."

"Do you need a drink?" she said, and Alan nodded.

Rachel found the staff-nurse in the kitchen where he was pouring out a protein yoghurt. She checked his name tag.

"Is it Stephen or Steve?" she asked.

"Steve." He smiled and would have shook her hand but was still busy pouring. "We're hoping Alan will eat more soon. His swallow reflex is improving," Steve said. "Do you know about his nightly trips?"

Rachel shook her head.

"Alan's been sneaking off with your grandmother. Motorbike trips into the hills, rowing across midnight lakes and picnics in spring meadows. They've had quite a month."

"Is that allowed?" Rachel asked.

"We encourage the patients to explore and go outside the formal training program. That's why VEEP was designed as an open-world environment."

"He seems to believe VEEP is real. I mean it's just a computer game, right?"

Steve nodded. "The difference is that we use CRF-23, which helps people suspend belief. It's based on the chemical your brain releases at night, which is why weird stuff can happen in your dreams and seem real. We use it to make VEEP feel genuine. It's not uncommon for patients to find it more rewarding than reality. They have more mobility, and we design it from their past, so it feels like home."

"That's reassuring, thanks." Rachel said.

"You really care, don't you?" Steve commented. "Not everybody does."

***

Most of the time, her Grandad slept. Rachel found it hard to talk to him, with such a one-sided conversation. She wasn't sure if she should talk about her new flat, or the challenge of finding a decent single man in Molesey, or reminisce about favourite family subjects. Her Grandad's right hand moved up and down the tubes at the side of his bed, occasionally taking a tight grip of the tube and twisting back and forth rhythmically, even when he had his eyes shut. As the visitor hour shrank, she kissed him goodnight and moved on to the next bay.

"Hi Grandma!"

"Rachel, come here and give me a hug. I love you so much," she said.

"You seem very perky Grandma."

"Hot date tonight!" she declared, and Rachel had a sinking feeling.

"We're heading out in a Triumph Stag."

"Is that a motorbike?"

"Oh no, it's an open top sports car, beautiful. Nothing like the sea breeze in your hair on a summer's day." Her Grandma smiled.

"I'd better leave you to get ready," Rachel hugged her Grandma extra tight as the visitor bell rang a final warning.

"Give him a kiss from me," Rachel said.

***

It was a thunderous sky and the rain was threatening to break at any moment. Staff-nurse Steve had accepted an invitation to the double funeral, even though members of the clinical team rarely attended such events. He was hoping to find Rachel and talk to her privately now that she no longer had a reason to come to the hospital. Steve managed to find Rachel alone in the garden, away from the attention of the other mourners.

"It's not uncommon for a husband and wife to die soon after each other. I think they would have approved," he said softly.

"Perhaps they're still together," Rachel said.

"I hope so," he said.

"What's it like? Inside VEEP?" she asked.

"It's like any computer environment," he replied. "Of course, it's different for the clinical staff because we don't take the drug. We need to keep a medical perspective."

"I'd like to have seen them together," Rachel mused.

"They were very much in love. I can tell you that."

They stood in silence for a few moments, and the nurse cleared his throat.

"Listen," he said. "A group of us are going cliff-diving on Sunday. It's the one they used as the model for the VEEP course. It makes you realise what it must be like, the fear and the ecstasy. It's the closest you can get to VEEP, without taking the drugs. Would you like to come?"

Rachel hesitated.

"We could grab a bite to eat afterwards?" he said.

***

The sea was turquoise. The staff-nurse seemed more relaxed to Rachel, away from the hospital, more comfortable somehow, in her presence. They were doing pencil jumps.

"We'll do it side by side," Steve said.

"One!" laughed Sanchez, relishing his turn in the instructor role.

Rachel and Steve walked to the cliff's edge.

"Now separate a bit. You don't want to be too close."

They both took a pace to the side.

"Two."

Rachel watched Steve raise his hands and copied.

"Three."

Rachel steepled her hands.

"Go!"

Steve disappeared over the cliff. Rachel froze.

"Go!" Sanchez shouted again.

Rachel pushed-off into the air, terrified. She remembered to go stiff like a plank of wood as she'd been told, but rigid would be a better description. She closed her eyes as she hurtled towards the waves and felt the shock as she pierced the sea. Bursting through the surface she gasped and swivelled around to find Steve. He lifted her bodily out of the water and dropped her back again, shrieking. The water was golden, scattering the light into dazzling pieces.

They swam to a rock shaped like a turtle's back and clambered out. The other divers gave her a round of applause and she did a mock curtsy.

"That was amazing!" Rachel said.

"Would you do it again?"

She laughed. "May be, but once is enough for today!"

Sanchez was on the cliff top, shouting. Steve cupped his hand to one ear, indicating that Sanchez should shout louder.

"EMT on ward!"

Steve turned to Rachel. "We need to get back," he said.

"I thought you were off duty?" Rachel asked.

Sanchez's voice carried over the crashing waves, "Pull your green toggle," she heard him say. One by one the others on the rock vanished, until there was just Rachel and Steve left.

"You didn't realise, did you?" he said. "You were back at our first date."

"I'd forgotten."

"We've had a wonderful life together, Rachel. This is not how it ends."

He reached over and placed the green toggle from his suit in her hand. She slowly pulled out the cord of her toggle and offered it to him.

Two pops fired together like the corks of champagne bottles, echoing against the cliff. The waves lolled against the empty rocks.

Made In Morocco

Tyre-marks snake away in several directions, but there's nothing you could call a road. The tracks weave amongst large, wheel-bursting rocks that have increased in size and frequency in the past hour. I glance down at the meaningless instructions and then stuff them into the car door pocket.

"Try over there," I say, pointing.

We already know that a desert isn't made from postcard-pretty sand dunes. It's a bleak zone of vast, unknown dimensions, filled with obstacles to wreck your plans. A place where dreams shrivel and die. We've navigated across many such regions, and both carry the scars. A desert by literal definition is empty, devoid of any help, although you may see a few mirages. Eventually, you must find your own way out, if you can. This time we get lucky. A building separates from the horizon, and we finally pull into the hotel. We are weary, with only an hour before our excursion starts, an adventurous camel ride into the Sahara. I'd rather be curled on the hotel bed. The receptionist greets us with a familiar refrain.

"Welcome! Your first time in Morocco? I hope it will not be your last!"

We nod and smile as much as two bone-tired, sad people can do.

"Do you have a hat?" he asks. This is a new question. Puzzled, we both answer yes.

"Let me see," he says.

I pull out a beige thing that makes me resemble an ageing cowboy and Gill produces a more stylish item. The receptionist waggles a finger.

"These are not hats for the desert," he declares.

Ten minutes later, we're being driven down a dusty street to a non-descript house that doesn't resemble the tourist shop I expected. Our driver opens the car door. The sun is so bright that everything feels washed-out and colourless, or perhaps that's just me. We're ushered inside the house and while my eyes take a moment to adjust, my mind takes longer. The walls are aquamarine; the ceiling is red with thousands of green and white leaf motifs. On every patch of wall hangs an astonishingly colourful item. I see plates of all styles, in colours that range from brilliant sun-yellows to the purples that lurk behind distant mountains. There are pistols that deserve to belong with highway robbers, and daggers possessing blades that curve in sudden and peculiar ways, a curled tip or a lightning-fork zigger, next to three bottles surely designed to hold genies. Plus teapots — fifty or sixty antique silver teapots tilted at jaunty angles, ready to pour. Sitting on a low bench amongst this treasure is a Berber in a multi-shaded blue outfit. He's dark-skinned, with an English-villain moustache and a broad smile. Swiftly, he greets us and offers a Berber Whiskey, as he calls the mint tea. While we wait for our piping hot glasses to cool, he explains the regional varieties of turban, the technique for wrapping and tying the material, and how the female version is more complex owing to the tassels.

I find it strange that the turban is simply an elaborate scarf wrapped around your head. I always imagined it was a ready-made hat for hot days that you simply lifted on or off at your whim. I fall in love with a blue-shaded variety, and we haggle peacefully over a low price that feels like a bargain.

"Look," he says once we have concluded the deal. Reaching into a dark recess in the wall, he produces a leather chest. He lifts the lid — not enough for us to see completely inside, and begins to pull out jewellery, which he lays on a cloth. Piece after piece emerges, mainly silver items encrusted with gems. He asks what we like, and we explain very clearly that we're not looking for jewellery. Within minutes Gill wears a stunning sunburst necklace that we both adore.

"How much?" I ask.

A set of old-fashioned scales appear from the recess. The necklace is delicately placed on one side, and a series of weights are tested on the opposite cup until the scales balance.

"Silver is priced by weight," he tells us.

That's a shame, I think, since it doesn't take into account the art, treating jewellery as a commodity. A short discussion over dirhams follows.

"You've made an excellent choice," he tells us. "This symbolises fertility, and good fortune. I am glad you chose it."

I'm cynical. The leather pouch of powdered reindeer-horn hanging over our bedpost has proved fruitless. The John Radcliffe Clinic with their modern expertise in IUI and IVF have quietly removed us from their register. The herbalist at the Wellbeing Centre continues to mix very expensive potions that can repair anything, except us. Yet there's something about this wild den of colour and treasure that lets me dream. Magic may have deserted us, but if any fragments remain, this is where they would be found, on the edge of the Sahara where the horizon is a smudge in the haze.

***

The two camels lurch through the orange-walled alleys of the town, hidden back ways we must traverse to reach the alluring sands promised by the travel brochure. Palm-tree fronds split the sun into a complex mosaic of light, making a tapestry on the ground that disguises the trash, a dead cat, the detritus of poverty that our camels step over stiff-legged, as we peer from above. Leaving the town, I abandon my final hopes for a child of our own and let the heat wash over me.

My two-toed camel sways as it picks its way through barren rock fields encircling the town. Red-gold sand swirls in the wind, creating patterns like a kid's kaleidoscope toy. My camel stops to chew at a tuft of yellow grass stems, miraculously releasing the smell of fresh pine forests. We ride, at a comfortable, rhythmic pace, through heat and dust. The turban is perfect, like something I've always worn, practical and totally natural. Talking requires effort, so Gill and I fall into a companionable solitude. I run a hand across my camel's neck to soak in the cut-straw texture, ready for a spark to ignite. Soon I'm in a trance, rocked by the lullaby steps of my camel, and lost in worlds that might-have-been.

***

We reach our destination, amongst sand dunes of astonishing colour and splendour. The scene is the very image of Arabian nights from ancient tales. The light is so strong that it appears to be layered on the ground. Our camels wander freely while we sit on a rug. The smell of mint reaches us from the burbling teapot, where Ali keeps busy. I stare at a distant line of palm trees above a wall of rock, and mountains.

Ali walks over with his fast smile and lifts the silver kettle high to pour heavily-sugared tea into our doll-sized cups. If we rode for fifty days, he told us earlier, we would reach Timbuktu. I imagine a line of Berbers in striking blue outfits decorated with crescent moons and stars, kneeling and praying in dedication, with camels meandering behind, aimlessly. I would be with the camels.

Over the top of a dune appear two large SUVs. We watch doors slam, and an array of men, in rags that seem to be wound independently around each limb, shout and cajole each other in a tongue we can't translate. They form a staggered line and walk towards us, coming at an angle to slow their descent down the crumbling face of the dune. Each man carries something at his side or slung over a shoulder.

"Are those guns?" Gill asks.

Ali comes to top-up our drinks.

"These are the gnaou," he says. "Music and food."

The men wave as they walk past, the guns now revealed to be musical instruments.

"Relax," Ali says. "We will prepare."

***

The sun has almost set when Ali gestures us over. He brings us to an open-faced tent, which has until now kept its back turned to us. I see a low table, with cushions along one side. The table is spread for a banquet. There is torn bread and fresh fruit in every primary colour; figs, oranges, berries, limes and peculiar pods and bounty that I can't name. It seems impossible that all of this food could be for one couple. Ali indicates that we should sit, to face the desert and four empty stools. The gnaou emerge, carrying instruments. Two have drums, and a nearly toothless man in the middle carries a battered lute-like instrument with twelve strings. It has two sound holes, each filled with an elaborate filigree design in white, that would look at home decorating a Casbah window.

They begin to play. The leader thumps out a rhythm on the side of his instrument and begins singing once the drums have picked up his lead. He strums and picks at the battered lute, and is really, really, good. What's more, he's enjoying himself. He smiles, and laughs as he picks out complex runs, before bursting into another line,

"Lay-la-lay-la-leek," he sings.

The wine flows more freely than mint tea as the sky shifts to a darker palette.

When the music is over, we wander hand-in-hand towards our tent. I watch a lone beetle scurrying over the sand, as though looking for an elusive entrance to a different world. Or perhaps the beetle knows its place, I think, and we're the ones searching. Our tent contains a wide bed covered in white linens and scattered with rose petals. There are subdued lights in each corner, and the coarse tent material arcs low over the bed, billowing slightly as the night winds pick up their pace. Quietly, we undress. We don't talk about our journey here, of decisions taken, dead-ends, tragedies, paths that are closed. Those are gone, and we've agreed to share the way forward together. Abandoned worlds weigh heavy though, dragging behind us on chains of hope, scouring deep channels where pain and resentment may sweep in when the next storm arrives.

Before clambering into bed, Gill removes the silver necklace and lays it down like a talisman. For the first time in many years we have no overriding goal, no shared purpose. We hold each other, kiss, and silently celebrate life. Sleep rapidly overtakes us, and I dream of laughter, the elusive, raucous sound of a child wanting to be chased. The laugh is fading, and although my legs feel heavy and lethargic, I keep running as fast as possible, because that's all I can do.

***

The morning is cold. I'm tired, and my body is worn from yesterday's journey, and yet my limbs feel loose, as though a hard shell has broken and fallen from around me. We're soon on our way back to town. As we lope into the alleyways, I see the shadow of our camel train silhouetted on the wall, a picture-book image of myth, Lawrence and Scheherazade, fashioning their personal legends with courage, underwritten by loss. Their narratives were wonderful, but I'm not so sure it felt that amazing to them as they took each treacherous step. It's only with hindsight that our random interactions gain meaning. Like these alleys — they follow strict geometric designs, absolute lines, or a perfect parabola, but wandering across them, the lanes criss-cross each other so the plan is only visible to Allah.

Two dogs harry the camels for a game, retreating to their territory when marauding children take over.

"Un stilo?" Three kids yell.

A smaller girl looks up as we pass, "Bon-bon," she says, more a demand than a question. I have some in my pack, but they're unreachable. I would like to give her them all and share in the feeling of compassion that rides with me today. Ali shoo's the children away, with good grace, and they giggle at some joke he makes. Berber women, in black regalia with gold trimming, carry bulging bags on backs or heads, burdened as any mule, but laughing as they talk. Other women sweep red dust from the boundaries of their dwelling. They acknowledge us graciously, and we smile back.

Too quickly, we arrive at the hotel, which seems far more like civilisation than it did yesterday. With a shudder, the camels fall to their knees at Ali's bidding, and collapse on haunches to shed their tiresome loads. Ali sings gently to them. I swing reluctantly off my camel's back and give her one last affectionate rub. We tip Ali and thank him profusely, before moving towards the cool air of our hotel.

I have a strange sensation that the world has shifted, a subtle change that I can't place or name. Gill smiles at me, and somehow, I'm aware that she feels it too. I hesitate, and wonder if speaking my thoughts would be a curse, and then I hear Ali one last time. I'm not certain whether he speaks to the camels or me. Perhaps his message is for everyone.

"Sch, sch," he whispers. "All is well."

***

Dedicated to Freya.
Born in 2004. Made in Morocco.

Acknowledgements

'Fragile'
first published by *The Writer Magazine USA*, 2016

'Blue Monsters'
first published by *Momaya Press* in the *Utopia/Dystopia Short Story Review*, 2017

'This is not how it ends'
first published by the *H G Wells Short Story Competition Anthology*, 2017

'Time travel for 11-year olds'
first published in issue 9 of the magazine *Firewords*, 2017

'Wild Animals'
first published by the *Rattle Tales Group* in *Rattle Tales*, 2018

'The King's Men Vigilantes'
first published in the magazine *Flying South*, 2018

'Other People's Wives'
first published in *Ambit*, 2018

'368 Friends'
first published by *InkTears*, 2018

'Gingerbread'
first published by *Popshot* magazine, 2019

'Made in Morocco'
first published in audio format by *The Drum*, 2019

'Shadow Day'
first published by *Momaya Press* in the *Trading Places Short Story Review*, 2019

'Mutilated Gods'
first published by *Popshot Magazine*, 2020

'Race for the Pot'
first published in the magazine *Flying South*, 2020

'Laughing at Funerals'
first published in the magazine *Flying South*, 2020

'The Flavours of Savannah'
first published in the magazine *Flying South*, 2020
nominated for a *Pushcart Prize*

A Note From The Author

Most of these stories were published in a variety of magazines and journals between 2016 and 2020, although many were written several years earlier, often inspired by events that took place a long time before that. It has been on my mind to gather them together into a collection for several years, but the pace of life and pressures of work, have kept me away from that process. In 2020 I did publish a non-fiction book, *Questions — A User's Guide*, which tied into my day job on Artificial Intelligence (AI) at SWARM Engineering and was an asset rather than a distraction from work. As an executive at a venture funded company, I am acutely aware of the attention that is paid to your activities, in and out of work, and never wished to give any cause for concern that my focus was not fully devoted to the success of the company. In the last few months, several events among our family and friends forced me to reflect on mortality, and since none of us know how long we have been allotted, I decided I really should make the effort to publish these stories while I am in the fortunate position of being able to do so. Simultaneously, we secured additional funding and executive support for SWARM, which allowed me to take some free time over the winter holiday to rapidly edit and sequence these tales, ready for publication.

    Since these stories were originally written, we have seen the rapid rise of generative AI tools that can suggest new ideas, write, and edit material. Even though I work in this industry, I have been astonished at the amazing capability of these products, and the pace at which the tools are improving. I am an avid user of AI tools in my day-job, and I know how much value they can bring. I believe many books will soon be either created, and/or substantially edited with AI tools. I would be a hypocrite to say that I disapprove of this process, as I welcome new technology and love to adopt it and encourage others to use it. However, another key reason to publish now was to highlight that these stories were the work of my own hand and mind. Perhaps I will come to regret this decision, and my third collection will include stories that were a heavy collaboration between myself and an AI writing partner, and I will look back at these tales as the mere scribblings of an inexperienced human author. Even so, I wanted to put a stake in the ground before the distinction between human and AI creativity became more blurred.

There are plenty of stories that didn't make the cut for this collection, because I felt they had not yet earned their place, and I wanted to include only those that held a special meaning for me. A few have already aged a little — when 368 Friends was originally written it seemed shocking that a person could have that many friends on social media, while today people count their followers by the thousands or more! I didn't change it, as the story is an insight into the way the world was evolving, and the emotional core of the tale remains relevant. Some of the included stories are deeply personal, others gather old friends, while many more combine and merge different places, people, and experiences into a lesson or journey that was not so obvious as the events unfolded in the real-world. Narrative is a wonderful tool, and it functions especially well with hindsight.

I can tell you that I did frequently use time-travel when I was eleven, on my way to and from Banbury School (and Wild Animals gives an accurate description of that exact route) but the railway bridge in the Time Travel story is stolen from behind my grandparent's house in Blackpool, and the story starts at a New Year's Eve party I once attended at a friend's house in Morden. As I said, many of the narratives blend people and places in a way that seems perfectly natural in my mind, as they are connected for reasons I cannot always explain. The Twaddlers of Newport Beach reflects the sights and sounds of a walk and bike ride I took more than ten years ago on Balboa Island in Southern California, but was mostly inspired by the person I saw at the end of that day, who was buying the precise elements described in the opening scene, which made me curious as to why they had been purchased and where they were going. The story was simply a way to capture the atmosphere of that day and solve the puzzle.

    Locations are sometimes chosen because I can recall them with sharp clarity. Crouch Hill outside Banbury is the setting for The King's Men Vigilantes, with a little of the Rollright stones thrown in for good measure, two places that dominated my childhood summers, and which I can return to in my imagination at any time. Various work colleagues lurk in these stories, sometimes because they were an intricate part of events, or because I know them well and it makes the writing process easier to place someone familiar into a new setting, to see how they might react. There are a handful of relatives and several close friends in these tales, and a gardener I know gets a starring role in one story, as does the wonderful man who used to walk our dog. While many stories were sparked from an idea, or a snippet of conversation, or a brief memory, Wild Animals was deliberately written for a competition based on a prompt of 'rain', and I had no idea what to write. My friend Mark told me that when he thought of rain, he recalled many days walking home from school — which catapulted me into the same scenario. There are also a few stories inspired by Simon, who featured frequently in the collection *Nobody Will Ever Love You* and is now beginning his own creative writing journey — I am looking forward to reading his perspective on our teenage adventures!

There are too many people involved in a collection such as this to thank everyone individually. There are those that have been involved in the process of forming, inspiring, reviewing, or actively participating in these stories, unwittingly or not. My brother and sister, Alan and Anne, continue to read and provide constructive criticism that is always welcome, as do my wife and daughter, Gillian and Freya. I am permanently indebted to every editor or publisher that selected one of my stories for publication in their magazine or journal. More than anything, I am thankful to every person who takes time to read these scribbled ideas of a human, and I hope you can find something to connect with that relates to your own life. A sentence, an image, a concept, a memory, a friend or place — if these stories bring any of those back to your conscious thoughts and let you reflect on some aspect of your life, then I will have succeeded in my task. Writing is the closest thing we have to telepathy and is the best way to understand how others truly think, but it takes two people to establish the connection. Thank you.

Questions For A Book Club

If you're interested in discussing these short stories in a book club, here are a few questions to kick-start your discussion:

1. What do you think are the key underlying themes that run through this collection?
2. In certain stories, such as Fragile or Time Travel for 11-year-olds, there are several possible interpretations for the ending. Should the writer have given more hints about the interpretation they imagined, or is it good to leave that up to the reader to decide?
3. If one of these short stories were the first chapter of a novel, which one would you most want to carry on reading? Why?
4. Which was your favourite story, and is that different from the answer you gave above?
5. The stories are written in a mix of first person (I did this…) and third person (she did that…). Did you find one style more effective than the other?
6. The narrators in the first-person stories vary from male to female, young to middle-aged. Did you feel the writer was able to express each voice correctly?
7. Several stories ultimately had a positive outcome — such as Wild Animals, Mutilated Gods, or Made in Morocco, while others were open-ended (e.g. End of the World), and a few were negative — like Gingerbread. How did the endings change your feeling towards the stories?
8. The settings in the stories are very diverse. How did the author use them to support the story, and was there a particular setting that stood out for you?
9. Which story has the most potential to be turned into a

movie? Why?
10. What was the most powerful emotional connection in this collection, that moved you to laugh, cry, or stop and think about your own life?

Nobody Will Ever Love You

by A M Howcroft

Short stories are like miniature films, and this prize-winning collection by A M Howcroft delivers a potent screening of art-house tales and Hollywood blockbusters. They are studded with a memorable cast of characters, such as a chicken-factory worker balanced high on a slippery roof, a woman carving saints out of driftwood, teenage boy-racers who've solved life's mysteries, through to a business woman who dies nine times. Each story is set within a rich-cinematic backdrop to reveal people at critical turning points, with delicately balanced risks and rewards. Whether starting riots in Paris, breaking into a friend's house in California, or killing time before being busted by customs officers, the narrators are flawed, unpredictable, smart and stupid in equal measure. Funny, moving and often provoking, these compelling stories will entertain; giving you images that linger and dialogue you'll want to repeat in fake accents.

An exciting new talent who really knows how to write and keep the reader thoroughly engaged.

Katie Fforde

Intellectually stimulating, funny and poignant, his work is full of new ideas, invention and philosophical what-ifs.

David Gaffney

Author of Swan-off Tales, Aromabingo

Questions — A User's Guide

by A M Howcroft

Everybody asks questions, of their friends, colleagues, lovers, and themselves. Yet how many of us have been trained to do it effectively? There are techniques used by professions; teachers, psychiatrists, lawyers and salespeople are all taught about the art and science of questioning, but their approaches vary greatly based on their differing goals. With the explosion of so called big-data, organisations are now using powerful software tools to ask questions and analyse or influence our behaviour. This book takes you on a mind-blowing ride through the history and techniques of questioning, looks at the heroes and villains, the technology and the future of the questioning industry. Whether you want to triple your sales revenues, avoid questions that will damage your relationships, or simply lead a happier life, this book can be your guide. You will find out how questions are used in Hollywood movies, why they are critical to jokes, and the ten most bizarre things you might get asked at an interview. We will blow the cover on how people use bias to make us answer questions a certain way, and you will learn new skills such as the art of using silence effectively, or how to spot hooks and use them to great effect. You can discover how to become a guru, and we will expose the way questions can change your memories. You may even learn how to master the black art of the killer question.

This book is fascinating. You'll never think of questions in the same way ever again.

Susan Bennett, the original voice of Siri

Printed in Great Britain
by Amazon